JEAN RICHEPIN

THE BULL-MAN
AND
THE GRASSHOPPER

Translated and with an Introduction by
BRIAN STABLEFORD

THIS IS A SNUGGLY BOOK

ISBN: 978-1-943813-66-7

Contents

Introduction

"UNE HISTOIRE DE L'AUTRE MONDE" [A Story of the Other World] by Jean Richepin, here translated as "The Bull-Man and the Grasshopper"—because the original title would be somewhat misleading nowadays—was by far the longest item in the author's first collection of fiction, *Les Morts bizarres* [Bizarre Deaths] (1876). It was reprinted in *Quatre petits romans* [Four Short Novels] (1882), and eventually issued in isolation in 1919.

Jean Richepin was born in Medea (now Lemdiyya) in Algeria in 1849. He was the son of a military surgeon, and lived a peripatetic existence in his early years, before the family settled in northern France, where Richepin went to school in Douai before going to Paris in 1868 to study at the École Normale Supérieure. According to the accounts he gave when he became an habitué of the Bohemian cafés of Montmartre, he had been a brilliant student who graduated from the École in 1870 with flying colors, but with a severe dose of disenchantment; other accounts suggest that he left without taking a degree. Either way, he made no attempt to obtain the teaching post for which students at the college generally aimed, and later claimed to have embarked on a career of adventure instead, serving with distinction during the Franco-Prussian War as a sharpshooter.

Whether the latter claim is true or not, Richepin was not in Paris during the brief rule of the Commune, which he would probably have joined if he had been—he was infected with revolutionary ideas by the Communard propagandist Jules Vallès, of whom he subsequently wrote a biography—and might well have ended up being transported to New Caledonia. The subject-matter of "Une Histoire de l'autre monde" thus had some personal relevance to him.

When Richepin reappeared in Montmartre again in the mid-1870s he rapidly became well-known for his flamboyant style of dress and behavior. Although he was acquainted with the members of Émile Goudeau's Hydropathes, and became a regular at the Le Chat Noir, where the club in question was reformed after a brief hiatus—he loved to sing there to Maurice Rollinat's piano accompaniment—he was never seen as a member; Félicien Champsaur remarked that Richepin was the Hydropathes' most important inspiration, far too important to be merely one of its crowd, but he was probably being sarcastic. At any rate, Richepin certainly wanted to remain distinct from any group, having the same mania for standing out from the crowd as his principal literary idols, Charles Baudelaire and Petrus Borel. Thus, although the heyday of his writing career developed in the context of a perceived contrast between the Decadent/Symbolist Movement on the one hand and Naturalism on the other, he made every effort never to belong to either camp.

Richepin's first collection of poems, *La Chanson des gueux* [The Song of the Vagabonds] (1876) was prosecuted for obscenity, just as Baudelaire's *Les Fleurs du mal* had been two decades earlier—a punitive oppression that gleaned angry protests from Victor Hugo and Gustave Flaubert, among others. The gain in notoriety was, however, balanced out by a heavy fine of five hundred francs, on top of a month's imprisonment, which left him in dire straits for some while. The censored passages of *La Chanson des gueux* were not restored until 1964, long after Richepin's death in 1926. Not unnaturally, however, the author's reaction to their excision was combative, and the themes and language of his poetry remained extreme, especially in the erotically-charged *Les Caresses* [Caresses] (1877), the aptly titled *Les Blasphèmes* [Blasphemies] (1884) and *Mes Paradis* [My Paradises] (1895).

Richepin's first full-length novel, *Madame André* (1878) followed soon after the publication of collection containing the present novella, but he had a much greater success in 1881 with *La Glu* [Birdlime], whose title is employed metaphorically to refer to the adhesive capacity of a *femme fatale*; it was adapted for the stage in 1883, further adapted as an opera, with music by Gabriel Dupont, in 1910, and was filmed more than once. The gypsy romance *Miarka, la fille de l'ourse* [Miarka the She-Bear's Daughter] (1883) also enjoyed considerable success, and was also filmed. In the meantime, his short fiction made important contributions to the development of the *contes cruel*, his initial collection being followed by *Cauchemars* [Nightmares] (1892) and *Contes de la décadence romaine* [Tales of the Roman Decadence] (1898). He proved expert in adapting such work to newspaper feuilleton slots around the turn of the century, but his work of that kind was only belatedly collected in *Le Coin des fous: histories horribles* [The Lunatic Asylum: Horrible Stories] (1921; tr., along with items from *Cauchemars* and other sources, as *The Crazy Corner*) and *Contes sans morale* (1922).

The stage adaptation of *La Glu* was rapidly followed by the lyrical drama *Nana-Sahib* (1884, with music by Jules Massenet), in which the central role was played by Sarah Bernhardt. When the actor playing opposite Bernhardt fell ill, Richepin took over the role himself—to enormous public acclaim, at least in his account. Bernhardt paid him the immeasurable compliment of saying that he was "even odder and hammier than I am—that's why I love him." He continued to produce work for the stage in greater profusion than volumes of poetry or prose, some of it for musical accompaniment. His greatest popular success in the theater was *Le Chemineau* [The Vagabond, in a less insulting sense than *gueux*] (1897), which was the first of his works to be adapted for the cinema, in 1906, followed by three further versions. He did not take the central role in any of those films, but he did appear as a screen actor, along with Sarah Bernhardt, in *Mères Françaises* [French Mothers] (1917), and he played one of the key roles in the film version of *Miarka* (1920).

Richepin was a very prolific writer between 1880 and 1901—the two years in which the first and last of his numerous children were born—but after the turn of the century he slowed down considerably. The vitriolic quality of his writing also eased, as his politics shifted toward the middle-ground. That relative decline in his reputation as a heroic rebel against authority and orthodoxy reached a kind of peak in 1909, when he not only put himself forward as a candidate for election to the Académie, but won, beating Edmond Haraucourt and Henri de Régnier, probably as the result of an anti-vote against the latter, and thus joined the literary Establishment in no uncertain terms. His views and opinions became even more conservative thereafter, although his final novel *L'Aile* (1911; tr. as *The Wing*) was a heroic attempt to break new ground in celebrating the contemporary technological revolution and the scientific genius fueling it.

By that time, Richepin had traveled a long way from "Une histoire de l'autre monde," both artistically and ideologically, but that first novella, although manifestly apprentice work, does contain many signs of the flamboyance and enterprise that were to mark his career with such a dramatic independence. It does not feature the most bizarre of the bizarre deaths described in his first collection, but it is certainly a flamboyant and eccentric melodrama, which remains very readable.

The translation was made from the version of *Les Morts bizarres* reproduced on the Bilbliothèque Nationale's *gallica* website.

—Brian Stableford

THE BULL-MAN
AND
THE GRASSHOPPER

Voyages form Youth.
(*The Wisdom of Nations*)

I
Justice Does Not Play Games

JEAN PIOUX and Marius Mazuclard made a sensational entry to the court-martial.

Jean Pioux was a Hercules, and one divined that on seeing him—not that he was, like the majority of his peers, a formless mass of muscle and flesh, but strength was imprinted in all his movements. In the regular swing of his broad shoulders, the rhythm of his march and the slow aspirations of his huge chest, one sensed an admirably equilibrated machine. Habitually, he supported his left fist on his hip, and his formidable arm was detached from his body, showing its form beneath the sleeve like a bundle of knotted ropes.

In spite of that attitude, Jean did not *pose*. To be convinced of that, it was sufficient to look at his serene eyes and his placid face. In spite of his narrow forehead, his beard and his bushy, sturdy and curly hair, he did not give the impression of being a brute, nor a braggart. One would have thought it the head of a pleasant fellow, borne by the neck of a bull and framed by the mane of a black lion.

Marius was completely different from Jean. Sometimes he almost dislocated himself with contortions, inflations of the back and effacements of the chest, as if he wanted

to pass through a hole or slide between fingers. He seemed
paltry and was only thin; he was believed to be small because he shrank himself. He struck deformed poses and
could pass for a cripple. In reality, he was tall enough, thin
and wiry, as supple as an eel, as hard as a saw-horse and as
mischievous as a monkey.

There was nothing more bizarre than his head. He had
everything required to be ugly, but he was not. His long
and colorless hair resembled vermicelli. His pale face, more
wrinkled than a miserly pear, was agitated, pulled, pinched
and shriveled by perpetual grimaces. From that papier-
mâché backcloth a long nose stood out, terminating in a
ball, slightly reddened at the end. In sum, Mazulard's face
rather resembled a violently shaken cream cheese with a
raspberry in the middle. And yet he was not ugly! His yellow eyes opened so wide, so bright and so keen, sometimes
so profound and always so intelligent that one forgot the
form of the lamp on seeing the flame that was burning
therein.

They entered arm in arm, Jean provoking a movement
of admiration and Marius a burst of laughter.

The laughter dominated during the interrogation,
to which only Marius responded, while Jean contented
himself with approving everything his friend said with an
energetic gesture.

To the president's first question regarding name, age
and profession, they both straightened up and Marius'
voice was heard, sounding oddly like a corncrake. While
his lips advanced and retreated in all directions, his nose
trembled and his cheeks rippled like water under a gust
of wind, he pronounced loudly and in a single breath the
following sentence:

"Jean Pioux called the Bull-Man Marius Mazuclard called the Grasshopper thirty and forty mountebanks."[1]

They had only seen the grimaces, and had understood nothing at all. There was mention of a bull, a grasshopper, thirty, forty and a bank; what could all that mean?

"Repeat," said the president.

He repeated the same thing. They laughed louder, and did not understand any better.

"Explain yourselves!" said the colonel, who dared not join in with the general hilarity.

"Well, I said that my friend is named Jean Pioux and that people call him the Bull-Man because he's very strong. I said that my name is Marius Mazuclard, nicknamed the Grasshopper because I have spindly legs. I said that he's thirty and I'm forty. Finally, I said that we're mountebanks. Don't confuse us with bankers, by the way."

"Accused," replied the judge, biting his moustache in order not to laugh, "try not to make so many grimaces when you speak; one might think that you were doing it expressly to excite hilarity."

"Oh, that's a habit; it's my métier, you see."

"Your métier?"

"Yes, Mon Président. By profession I'm an acrobat, contortionist, conjurer, ventriloquist and grimacer. I'm an ape made man, and he's a statue in a blouse. We both teach all bodily exercises, such as point, counterpoint, cane, staff, Parisian and Marsellais kick-boxing, English

---

1 The word I have translated as "mountebanks" is "*banquistes*," which refers to fairground performers who perform in public. That was the original meaning of mountebank in English but it is nowadays used to refer more specifically to charlatans and con-men (as, in fact, is the French *banquiste*); I employed the word anyway in order to preserve the pun that Marius makes.

and French boxing and wrestling with flat hands, renewed from the Greeks and Romans, as was practiced in Greece and Romania, Boom!"

"We didn't ask you for all that. Put a brake on your volubility, and let's get back to your situation, which you're aggravating by your attitude. You're part of the insurgent bands, you and your friend?"

"Pardon me! It isn't in Paris that there were insurgents!"

With that, the interrogation was suspended. There was no need for further confessions or further evidence to condemn the two poor devils. In any case, what argument could they have put forward? They had served in the troops of the Commune, the fact could not be denied. Instead of denying it, they were proud of it. Their case was clear.

And yet, they were neither scoundrels nor even revolutionaries, those two acrobats. They were simply Parisians! Without any concern for politics, they had followed the current in which they lived, they had done what everyone else did. Did they know where they were going?

But none of those reasons had any weight before the court-martial. Jean Pioux and Marius Mazuclard were condemned to deportation.

II
Port-de-France and Montparnasse

"PORT-DE-FRANCE! Sentences of several years! Travelers for exile change trains!"

It was by that ironic phrase that Marius Mazuclard saluted New Caledonia. Then he turned to Jean Pioux.

"Who had the idea of calling this Port-de-France? It's quite simply cruel. He'd have been cleverer to call it Hors-de-France."

And as Jean Pioux only laughed with the corner of his mouth, Marius only made one grimace at him.

Then they looked at one another with tears in their eyes, well aware that the cheerfulness was fake. But it was, after all, the best remedy for their sadness; so, while Jean Pioux passed the back of his hand over his cheek, Marius shook his nose vigorously, from which a tear fell. Then they made a pirouette, arm in arm, and marched through the port with a firm step, singing the chorus of a Parisian song.

The next day they were interned, under the registration numbers 377 and 378.

There is no need to recount their first year of deportation. Imagine an ordinary prison camp, with its regulation labors, its prison food and its atrocious discipline, and you will have the regime to which all those reputedly dangerous convicts were subjected on arrival. Political prisoners are in that situation. It takes a certain time of assiduous good conduct and regular toil for one to pass successively from the fourth class to the third, and so on. The fourth class is the prison camp, a prison camp on an arid and rocky island, without any possible hope of escape: Toulon on a block of coral surrounded by sea. The third class is a prison camp on land, milder, healthier, where one is in the midst of one's fellows and not in the mid-ocean. The second class is formed of convicts whose labor is free and whose life alone is subject to daily surveillance. Finally, those of the first class have become veritable colonists. But at that class political deportees hardly ever arrive.

It was a hard thing for the two friends, the cruel captivity in the beginning. Gusts of the free air that they had drunk all their lives echoed in their hearts. Aftertastes of the Paris that they loved so much, the Paris they cherished like a mother, which they regretted so much—even the rain that fell there, even the mud through which one trudged—rose to their lips again.

The first three months were terrible. Jean would have died without Marius. His robust nature would have succumbed under the weight of sadness and memories. But the grimacer knew how to make a joke of the sadness and cheer up the memories. He had ingenious paradoxes.

"You see," he said, "sadness is good for the happy; it distracts them. But we have other things to do than listen to it."

After wit, their best consoler was work. They understood that in working they were conserving their health and gaining a little liberty. That thought, the activity of their life, and the amity that united them, the habit they had acquired of sharing all their joys and all their troubles, rendered the second trimester of their internment more bearable.

Their good conduct, their application and their inventive intelligence in many difficult circumstances were noticed, as well as the energy of the one and the good humor of the other. Their cheerfulness was also noted as a good point, for it was an encouragement for everyone. In brief, at the end of the first year, numbers 377 and 378, although political prisoners, were allowed to pass into the second class.

They were to have a portion of a field to cultivate in a sort of small suburb situated not far from Port-de-France, placed under the surveillance of Adjutant Barbellez.

The latter was a former mariner, an old man as hard as leather, who led men brutally, but who was led himself by his daughter Jeanne.

The little one, as he called her, had been brought up by an aunt in Paris, and the old man had sent for her after the death of the aunt. He now had a fixed position and he hoped before long to exchanged his silver-thread epaulette for an officer's epaulette, and as he had no family in France, he wanted to establish himself definitively in Port-de-France in order to make his future retirement pension bear fruit.

As for the little one, it would doubtless be forgotten that her father had been a prison guard and she would end up marrying some supercargo in the merchant navy or some enriched colonist.

In the meantime, she was the providence of the deportees, for whom she did her best to ameliorate her father's harshness. Everyone loved her. She was, in any case, a fine big girl, already a woman by age, because she was nearly twenty-five, but still a child in the gaiety of her character. Blonde and slim, with a rather pleasant but ordinary face, she passed for beautiful in the small society formed by guards, deportees and convicts. In the kingdom of the blind, the one-eyed are monarchs.

One morning, Père Barbellez said to her: "Little one, there are going to be two new birds in the cage. You can prepare your hemp-seed, but not too good. They're vagabonds that it's necessary to watch."

"What have they done, then?"

"Oh, they're dirty communards who insulted the court-martial. They're still dangerous, although their good conduct has allowed them to pass into the second class."

"However, Father, you're not going to receive them too harshly, eh?"

Barbellez frowned, tugged his large moustache, assumed his most forbidding expression, and replied: "I'll receive them as I ought to receive all enemies of society, that's all!"

"And what are their names?"

"I don't know."

At that moment, Jean Pioux and Marius Mazuclard arrived, conducted by a guard. On seeing them, Jeanne started with surprise and hesitation, as if she recognized them vaguely, and tried to recall their features.

In fact, for anyone who had known them previously, they had changed a great deal. Jean, with his hairless face, and Marius, deprived of his long stringy hair, were unrecognizable. Then, if labor had sustained them, it had also made them leaner, along with the vigorous sea air, which fortifies but also desiccates. Jean had become all muscle and

Marius all sinew. The former no longer had the beautiful plenitude of flesh that causes lovers of open-hand wrestling to swoon, and one could count the tendons in his wrist, banded like ropes. The other, whose entire body had once been formed like a knotted handkerchief, would now only have made half a handkerchief to do his turn.

They took off their caps on finding themselves before Barbellez and Jeanne.

"Aha! There you are, my lads," said the adjutant. "Famous good-for-nothings, aren't we? I-know-not-whats who amuse themselves mocking a colonel! It's said that we're behaving ourselves now. You know, it's necessary not to think that just because you've risen in class you can fold your arms, damn it! One doesn't shirk, with Père Barbellez!"

And he became animated, as if there were an argument, as if someone had tried to contradict him. However, Jean and Marius did not say a word. They had been warned. They knew that the old man began by "having a go" at the prisoners. The best thing to do was not to respond.

"Yes, yes!" continued the adjutant. "And Barbellez, that's me . . . salute! And this is Jeanne, my daughter, whom it's necessary to respect as the apple of my eye, damn it! That's understood! About turn, then, and quick march!"

As they obeyed that order, Jeanne stopped them in order to ask their names. The more she had considered them, the more she had remembered them, but she could not make her memory precise.

"Come on, reply," said the adjutant, addressing Marius. "What are your names?"

Suddenly, Jeanne's memory returned, and she cried: "It's the Grasshopper and the Bull-Man!"

The adjutant, Marius and Jean were stupefied by that unexpected occurrence, for which Jeanne was soon able to give them an explanation.

The old aunt, Madame Derson, in whose home in Paris she had been brought up until the age of twenty, lived on the Boulevard Montparnasse, not far from the Observatoire. She kept a little laundry there, in which Jeanne had spent her childhood and youth, without any other diversion than going on Sunday evening to the Closerie des Lilas, at the foot of the statue of Maréchal Ney, to see the performers and listen to the singers. So she knew by heart all the patter that was rattled off in the square, all the exercises that were performed there, all the acrobats that were seen there.

Most of all, she loved the Bull-Man and the Grasshopper. The Bull-Man frightened her more than he amused her; but what she adored more than anything else was listening to and contemplating the Grasshopper. That inexhaustible verve, the songs he sang, accompanying himself on a violin formed by three cords extended by a bladder, the conjuring tricks, the contortions, the ventriloquism, had all remained in her memory with the vivacity that renders the memories of childhood so precious and so dear. It had needed all the changes undergone by the body, the costume and the face of Marius for her to hesitate so long over recognizing him.

And she recounted all those things to her astonished father; she spoke about it with joy, with enthusiasm, almost with tears. She seemed to have rediscovered a friend. She had rediscovered all of her childhood.

"You see, Father," she said, coaxingly, "it's necessary to be good to them. If you knew what good moments they enabled me to spend when I was small! I only had that pleasure, you see. And then, it isn't possible that they've committed a crime. There's been a mistake. They're worthy fellows, you see! Acrobats as they were, in spite of their poverty, they were good to all their neighbors. I can still remember, once, when an old singer had set up next to them and no one came to listen to him, the Grasshopper said that that wasn't good, that it was ingrate to forget the old, and they worked for him. Another day, the Bull-Man nearly broke his back juggling with big twenty-pound weights, and the Grasshopper dislocated something cracking his joints, and all that to give a few sous to the child of a prostitute who had died. They were even charitable to the public. There was often no one around them because of the bad weather, or because no one had a sou that evening. There were only us children there, who had nothing in our pockets and could only pay them in applause. It didn't matter—they did their turns just the same, for nothing, to give us pleasure. Oh, I love them, and they deserve it!"

She spoke with such volubility that Barbellez did not have time to get a word in, or even to pull himself together. He could not believe his ears.

As for Jean and Marius, they were deeply moved, and did not know how to thank the young woman. Jean twisted his cap in his fingers with an embarrassed expression and Marius, without being aware of it, assumed tender expressions that recalled his finest grimaces.

The astonishment of Barbellez and the gratitude of the two acrobats knew no limits when Jeanne, after her vehement speech, suddenly held her hands out to the convicts, saying to her father: "And look, here's the proof that I love them. I want to shake their hands."

"What are you doing, wretch?" cried the adjutant.

Suddenly, Barbellez could no longer stand it. His little gray eyes were injected with blood while his eyelids blinked with a feverish rapidity like the wings of a dying fly. He was beside himself. And, not daring to vent his anger on his daughter, he struck out with the flat of his sword at Marius, who was next to her, and who leapt sideways.

"Go, go!" said Jeanne to the two poor devils. "He's too angry. I'll calm him down. Go with the brigadier; he'll take you to the fields. I'll come to see you there."

As she said that, she hastened to loosen the collar of old Barbellez, who had collapsed on a bench, his face blue and his neck stiff, stammering inarticulate oaths with a thick tongue.

III
How Amour Comes to Exiles

TWO days later, numbers 377 and 378 were completely installed in a little hut alongside the fields, and they had returned from working all day on their little plantation when they received a visit from Jeanne. She brought them a little money, two pipes and tobacco, and promised to come back.

As for old Barbellez, he was still furious; but Jeanne had made him understand that if he caused any difficulty for the two men, who did not deserve it, she would hold it against him mightily and would never speak to him again. He was therefore indecisive between his rage against the two deportees, on whom he wanted to avenge himself, and his weakness for Jeanne, whom he dreaded upsetting.

In the meantime, he remained neutral, searching for a means of harming the two poor devils without discontenting his daughter. He had resolved, in his strong head, to punish them severely for the first fault they committed, and gradually to demonstrate to Jeanne that those so-called innocents were vulgar rogues. In order to do that, he allowed her willingly to go to see them.

The more generosity she shows them, he thought, *the more they'll think that they're authorized to take liberties with the rules; they'll do something stupid; that will prove sufficiently to Jeanne that she's misplaced her affection and her concern. Then I'll get my own back.*

Thanks to that reasoning on the part of Barbellez, Jeanne was able to go to see her two new friends often. Almost every evening, when she had finished her charitable round among the other colonists, she came to spend an hour sitting on the wooden bench that marked the door of the miserable hut.

There, they talked about Paris, the beloved and regretted Paris, the familiar quarter, the Place de l'Observatoire, where they had seen one another so many times without knowing one another; about Louis the Lion who competed with Jean; about Bourguet the Joker who sometimes tried to match wits with Marius; and the Boulevard Montparnasse, with its fine tall trees, its guinguettes and its lively brasserie; and the seed-nursery where laughing young couples mingle with long files of little boarding-school girls clad in gray.

The entire rosary of memories was told like that, in charming conversations, full of bittersweetness.

Marius, as always, cheered up the conversations with his sallies. About everything and everyone, about the baker in the Rue Vavin, about Mère Eugène's restaurant, and Madame Derson herself, he knew amusing stories. He had remembered every word and every gesture that depicted people at a stroke. He imitated the speech of one, the gait of another. He made everyone live again in his pantomime.

Jean was less rapidly expressive, but from time to time he found one of those true words, one of those sincere ones, which replace an entire speech and go straight to the heart. His loyal and good nature was suddenly revealed, like a ray of sunlight shining through the mist.

Jeanne put all her soul into listening to them and replying to them. At the same time, she found confidants in
them for the joys and sorrows of her childhood. She told
them many things that she had never been able to tell anyone: about her early years, so harsh, under the guardian-
ship of the miserly old aunt, who did not understand and
did not like children; about her youth, almost etiolated by
isolation, the assiduous work every week, with no friends
and no amour; and, later, the long voyage in order to come
to join a father she did not know, and her suffering on
finding her father so ungenerous, so brutalized by discipline and drink.

And her regrets, her desires, her chagrins, her entire life,
gradually passed into the hearts of Jean and Marius. They
wept together, and their hearts melted as they held hands.

"Do you know," said Jean to Marius, one evening, "I
love her with all my heart, that little Jeanne."

"Bah!" said Marius. "Me too. That's the way it goes."

IV
A Competition Begins . . .

THEY did not sleep much the following night. They were thinking about Jeanne. Each of them was trying to convince himself that he alone was veritably amorous, and could really be loved.

It isn't possible, Marius thought, *that Jean Pioux can love her as much as me. Damn it! Jeanne isn't a twenty-kilo weight. What can he say to her? What can he do with her? And then, can she feel her heart stirred by him? After all, he's the Bull-Man. If he talked to her about amour she'd be frightened. I'm very stupid to torment myself.*

Marius is ridiculous, Jean Pioux said to himself. *What a joke! With a nose like his, to imagine that he might please a young woman! I can see the picture from here: Jeanne would laugh in the face of the grimacer. Anyway, is he really touched deep down? Can he love as seriously as me? It's not love that he feels, it's a crush. It will pass. I'm quite wrong to dwell on it.*

The agitation of their minds was betrayed by the agitation of their bodies. They could no longer remain still in their beds. Jean turned over from time to time, all of a piece, like a dog flipping over. Marius shivered incessantly, like a mouse in a trap.

But they both remained silent, in order not to appear tormented.

Marius was the first to allow his ill-humor to spill out.

"Come on! Why are you shifting like that? One can't sleep here. To hear you blowing as you turn over, one would think one were sleeping beside a seal."

"At any rate, that seal is better than the baboon who's talking to me."

"Baboon?"

"Yes, baboon!"

They got up, angrily. For the first time in their lives, they were arguing. Their quivering hands met in the dark. An iron hand gripped Marius' wrist, who dug his fingernails into Jean's neck. They began to fight.

"Let me go," said the Hercules, relaxing his fingers. "We're mad."

And they went back to bed, utterly ashamed.

"Listen," said Marius, after a pause. "I beg your pardon, my old Jean. I'm heartless, for having said stupid things to you."

"It's me who ought to beg your pardon. It's me who started to get angry. Tell me you don't hold it against me, Marius."

"Get away! Let's not talk about it any more. Or rather, yes, let's talk about it. Look, since yesterday evening we've been hiding from one another like children instead of looking one another in the face like men. Let's reason a little. You love Jeanne, don't you?"

"Oh yes."

"Me too. That's the problem posed. Let's try to solve it, damn it! Before knowing Jeanne, we loved one another more than anything in the world. You often made sacrifices for me, and I did the same for you. We never argued about which of us might be the better. Today, here's a third person we both love. Well, let her decide! We'll tell her to-morrow how it is, straight out. If she rejects both of us, so much the better. I'll console you and you'll console me. If she chooses, well, too bad for the one who's refused. He'll swallow his amour. But at least, not having been able to win a woman, he won't lose a friend. What do you say?"

"You're right. For myself, I swear to you to do as you say."

"I swear it to you too. Now, it's understood. Let's give one another a good handshake, from the bottom of the heart. And then, let's go to sleep. Getting up is tiresome."

V
A Twofold Declaration

THE following day, Jeanne found the two friends much changed.

Jean remained seated, without daring to raise his eyes. With his elbows on his knees, he was clearing out and stuffing his pipe mechanically. Marius walked back and forth with a jerky stride, beating time to his rapid steps on the end of his nose, which he contemplated without realizing that it caused him to squint.

Hmm! Hmm! thought the young woman. *Has my father done something to them, or have I caused them some pain?*

"Mademoiselle," Jean interjected, with a decisive expression, "It's necessary that . . ."

He blushed like a schoolgirl and stopped short.

"What are you trying to say, my good Jean?"

"It's something," said Marius, "Something that . . . well, in the end, Jean doesn't dare, but I'll tell you what it is. We perceived yesterday that . . . oh, in truth, Mademoiselle, I don't dare either."

"What is it? Why don't you dare to speak? I don't understand. Have you some reproach to make to me?"

"Oh, Mademoiselle!" they cried, drawing nearer to one another.

"It's a request, then?"

"Yes, yes . . . except that we're afraid of annoying you, that's all."

"That's very bad, what you're saying! How can you fear annoying me by asking me for something?"

"Oh," said Jean, "you'll think we're stupid."

"You'll think we're ridiculous," added Marius.

And both of them, with sobs in their throats: "You might not come to see us any more."

"Explain yourselves! It's now that you're being ridiculous. Speak, then! I promise you that I'll do my best to grant what you request, and if I can't do anything, we won't be any less good friends for that. Speak! I want it."

And, moving closer to them, she held out a hand to each of them.

Two similar puppets, activated at the same time, could not have acted more in unison than the two unfortunates did. Each seizing the hand that was held out to him, covering it with tears and kisses, they fell to their knees abruptly and stammered, in the same strangled voice:

"Mademoiselle, I love you!"

It would have been grotesque, if it had not been so touching. Jeanne felt no desire to laugh, for she saw that they were weeping.

In amour, it is only the first word that costs. Once the wave has broken, a tide of words is unleashed. And they very rapidly explained to Jeanne everything that they had to say to her: the passion of each of them, the previous evening's dispute, the agreement of the night.

"What you're proposing to me is very embarrassing," she replied. "Choose! Choose one or the other! What if I don't love either of you?"

Jean's lips pursed; Marius' nose twitched.

"Don't worry," she said, to console them. "I love you both. I love you with amity, that's certain, as much as one another. But as to amour, I haven't yet thought of that. Think about it! Suppose I loved one of you, how do you think I could tell him and prove it to him? You're not thinking, then, about my father? Remember his rage on the day that he saw that you had a part of my esteem and my affection? For me, you're honest men, and I wouldn't hesitate to put my hand in yours, my dear Jean, or yours, my dear Marius, and to take one of you for my husband. But in my father's eyes, you're criminals, convicts that he can beat if they displease him, imprison if they resist him, and kill if they defend themselves. How could I confess such an amour to him? It breaks my heart to think about it. At the pain I feel, I sense that I'm in love."

"Oh, thank you, thank you a thousand times!" they cried.

"But I beg you," she added, "don't press me. Give me time to reflect. Let me see first what I can hope for from my father. That's the first obstacle to overcome. If I succeed in that, I'll choose between you. But until then, I want to love both of you. Let's reserve the choice for later. And promise me that whatever happens, we'll always be friends. Once the choice is made, it's necessary, if my father is against me, for all three of us to fight him."

The night was already black when she left, saying to them that she was going to see a poor sick woman who lived some distance away in the fields.

VI
Where is She?

TWO days later, the whole little colony learned that Jeanne had disappeared.

On the first morning of that absence, Père Barbellez was not unduly worried. In fact, Jeanne often returned late and always got up with the sun. It sometimes happened that, having quit her father the evening before, after the evening meal, she did not see him again until lunchtime the next day.

Her absence at that hour began to torment him; he ate in a bad mood, but nevertheless with an appetite, and he drank his customary half-bottle of cognac after the meal.

"Bah!" he said, sipping from his little glass. "I'll find out what's happened when I make my round."

But his round did not reveal anything to him. His daughter had not been seen anywhere that day. That became serious. He began to get gravely worried. He was irritated, and growling like a guard dog. That evening, he administered an unmerited blow with his cane to the shoulders of more than one poor devil.

Jean and Marius, who were working in the fields, still knew nothing when they returned to their hut in the evening, so they went to bed tranquilly, thinking that Jeanne had not come that day because she had too much to do, or because the previous day's confidence had caused her too much emotion. It was only the following day, when they went to work again, that they learned with everyone else the news of the disappearance, which consternated them more than anyone.

They went to see Barbellez immediately.

He had spent a sleepless night, drinking in order to comfort himself, and he discharged on them all the rage that his anxiety, overexcited by alcohol, had given him.

"What do these two wretches want? Where's your authorization to speak to the adjutant? Ah! You come in here without a paper from your sergeant! What stupid animal let you in without asking you for your permit? I'll put him in the lock-up for a week! And you'll be in irons, God damn it!"

The unfortunates had not had time to get a word in. Fortunately, he paused for breath, and as he stood up, unsteadily, in order to strike them with his cane, Marius and Jean were able to say to him: "It's for your daughter!"

"What! My daughter! What does she have in common with you, my daughter? Load of vermin!"

"We have information that might help to find her."

"Information? Have you seen her? That's information that I don't have! Well, speak, then, damn donkeys, let's have your information!"

"Your daughter . . ."

"Mademoiselle your daughter, damn it!"

"Mademoiselle your daughter, is it really the evening of the day before yesterday that she went missing?"

"What does that have to do with you? Yes, the last time I saw her was the day before yesterday, at about four o'clock in the afternoon."

"Well, we saw her after that, in the evening. She left us at nine o'clock."

"Ah! You've seen her! I wonder why she went to see riff-raff like you. Anyway—and then?"

"Then she set out across the fields, and she told us that she was going to see Louison."

"Who's Louison?"

"The sick woman, number 518."

"And what else?"

"What else? But that's all we know. We came to tell you right away, thinking that it might be useful to you. It's our haste to render you a service that prevented us from asking the sergeant for permission. The sooner the better, and . . ."

"Leave me alone! What chatterboxes! Your information doesn't inform me of anything at all. Whether it was mid-day, four o'clock or ten o'clock that Jeanne disappeared, it doesn't make it any easier to find her, does it? Oh, you'll pay dearly for this, damn it!"

"But it isn't our fault!"

"Yes, it's your fault. You only had to go with her."

"But you know very well, Monsieur Adjutant, that no one can go out in the evening without permission."

"That's good! On the matter of permission, you don't always have yours. Very well, I'll make my report today to headquarters, and tomorrow you'll go to the island to see whether the camp-beds are eaten by termites. Go! It's your last day of working in the open air today. Enjoy the rest of it!"

And he added, in the ear of a sergeant: "Watch those two fellows for me all day. I'm leaving them free until this evening deliberately. I hope they'll do something stupid.

At the first resistance, the slightest attempt to run . . . you understand me, eh? Bang! A lump of lead in the noggin!"

The opportunity to carry out that order would certainly have been presented, if Jean had been alone. "Oh!" he said to Marius, between his teeth. "I've a strong desire to slap that sergeant, so that he'll blow my brains out."

"Would you like to shut up?" replied Marius. "Jeanne might be found between now and this evening. If she comes back, we're saved. Let's wait until this evening, and let's work all day as usual. Precisely because we're right ten times over, let's not put ourselves in the wrong."

They did as Marius wished.

The day was long and atrocious. Under the eye of the sergeant, who was watching them, they dared not allow the thousand thoughts that were whirling in their heads and torturing their hearts to appear on their faces. They worked with their heads down, their hands clenched and their minds in turmoil.

Thus, all misfortunes were falling upon them simultaneously. They were losing Jeanne: Jeanne, who was the sole reflection of the adored Paris that they would never see again; Jeanne, whom they loved because all their past revived in her and all their hopes for the future flourished in her. And at the same time, they were losing their poor share of liberty, so painfully purchased by a year of cruel submission and crushing labor. Oh, all of Jean's strength could not suffice to support that weight, and even Marius' cheerfulness saw its wings broken by that blow.

When evening came they felt their hearts swollen to bursting-point, on finding themselves for the last time beside the little bench where they had spent such good evenings with Jeanne.

"Poor Jeanne," sobbed Marius. "Where can she be?"

"Oh," said Jean, "if I knew, I'd already be there . . . and in an hour, I will be, for I know where she is! She's dead!"

"What are you saying? For myself, I believe she's been captured by the savages."

Jean shrugged his shoulders incredulously, and let himself fall on the bench heavily, as if wiped out.

A quarter of an hour later, he was woken from his collapse by a brief remark that Marius whispered in his ear:

"We have to go and look for Jeanne."

VII
Mazuclard the Landscape Painter

BEFORE saying that decisive word to Jean, Mazuclard had remained motionless for some time, planted as straight as a statue against the upright of the door-frame, contemplating the crepuscular landscape with a fixed gaze.

Before him, almost at his feet, was a salt-marsh bordered with rushes and covered in water-lentils, curly duckweed and nenuphar lilies with broad flat leaves.

In the inland direction—which is to say, on the other side of the marsh—stood an obscure mass, a dense thicket in the form of a dome, from which a stream emerged. The current came to expire with audible splashes on the smooth surface of the plants, which were like the scales of the marsh. That noise, emerging from that darkness, was reminiscent of some strange song, stammered by a mouth of shadow.

The dome was formed by interlaced bushes, climbing creepers, bushy trees, mangroves of various subspecies and carollias.[1] There was a mass of verdure there, from which a long and broad line of somber woods stood out, climbing

---

1 This is a mistake; *Carollia* is actually a genus of bats. It is not clear what tree the author might have in mind.

toward the interior of the island. It resembled a river of trees, whose waves accumulated at the bottom of a slope. In following the course of that forest to the horizon, the gaze reached the ultimate background of the scene, where the jagged silhouette of mountains stood out vaguely against the blue-gray of the sky.

All that appeared in the half-light of the evening through the vaporous veil of dusk, which heightened the somber masses with vigorous hues and enveloped the contours with a kind of tremulous mist.

While night was falling, the breeze from the sea was whistling through the rushes, the stream was gurgling and the toads were croaking softly on the water-lentils, Marius had considered all those things and had reflected profoundly.

It was then that he had said to Jean:

"We have to go and look for Jeanne."

Jean raised his head at that cherished name; but as he had lost all hope, he did not welcome that proposition with his usual enthusiasm. He looked Marius in the whites of his eyes as one looks at someone who is mocking you, or a lunatic whose obsession has just become manifest. And he replied, in a slow and discouraged voice: "You know very well that's impossible."

Was it, in fact, possible to escape?

It was necessary no longer to think about escaping by day, since they would be on the island tomorrow.

To escape by night was folly. Anyone abroad by night in the authorized territory was sure to be hit by a bullet before he had taken a hundred paces. There were guard-posts everywhere. One of the largest was on the edge of the marsh, overlooking the cabins among which Jean and Marius had theirs.

Jean made all these objections in one minute, and fell back into his dejection.

"Listen to me, then!" said Marius. "I'm not mad, and I'm not making fun of you, as you seem to believe. Look a little, my worthy Jean Pioux, look over there, in the far distance, opposite the sea. What do you see?"

"Well, it's a mountain, of course. I can see it even better than in broad daylight," the other replied, with chagrin.

"And there, close by, what's that on the water of the marsh?"

"Black plants, which are motionless by day and on which the toads swarm by night."

"Good. And do you also see that stream, which enters into the black plants?"

"It emerges from under the trees, of course. But what does all that have to do with what you said to me just now? You're talking, like an imbecile, about going to look for Jeanne—which is to say, going to catch the moon—and then you're making me look at weeds and water. You're annoying me, in sum. Look at this, look at that! One would think you were spouting patter. Look, Messieurs, do you see this ball, this cup, this pocket? Well, hey presto, I'm going to make it disappear! Is that what you want to do?"

"Yes. I want to make something disappear, you hear? I want to make us disappear. And the cup that will hide us, old chap, is the weeds, the water and the trees. And the pocket where we'll find ourselves, is the mountain. Do you understand? It's quite simple. It's a matter of getting from here to the marsh unseen. Then, from the marsh to the stream, it's necessary to have the courage to submerge ourselves to up to the mouth in that ditch, in the middle of the viscous weeds and the toads crawling on top. It'll be long and sickening, but it's necessary."

"Keep going," replied Jean. "I'm following. I understand as far as the stream—but once there, what do you do?"

"I walk along the stream, under the trees; for the stream obviously follows the trees. For a start, it's like that everywhere in the world. Secondly, consider that the savage name for stream in this country is *Diaot*, and that *Diaot* signifies both water and shade. So the water is always in the shade, that's my reasoning. Another proof that it's true is that it's always cold. I conclude from that that if we get as far as the stream, we only have to go up it through the thicket. That will be harder than in the marsh. For one thing, it's very cold; and then, in places the branches will be at water level and it will be necessary to duck under them; and finally, I don't know what animals there might be in there. But in sum, too bad! You see the plan, don't you? With our four days of food supplies, which we collected yesterday, we keep going. We'll need that time to reach the mountain. Once we reach the mountain, my lad, we're free. And once we're free, we'll go find Jeanne."

"Marius, come here so I can kiss you!"

"As for savages," added Marius, laughing, "If they catch us, we'll do the act—that will amuse them."

"As long as they don't put us on a spit?"

"What do you expect. War is war. He who risks nothing gains nothing. If they eat us, well, we'll at least have the consolation of saving that we ran away at the risk of . . . the fork!"[1]

And with that, they made their preparations.

Ten o'clock chimed. Lights out! The clarion sounded at the blockhouse in Port-de-Prince; the reply came from the bay. The final note trailed away vibrantly in the darkness.

---

1 The French *fourchette* [fork], can also refer to a gallows.

No longer any light in the town, except in the guard-room, the red windows of which resemble watching eyes.

The hut of numbers 377 and 378 is plunged in a profound silence.

There is movement there, however, and no one is asleep. But everything is done without a sound. Marius is in the process of fitting a long sack laden with biscuit, rice and fava beans to Jean Pioux's back. He is carrying a smaller sack himself, also full of food. Above it, almost behind the head, is a packet wrapped in tarred cloth; that is tobacco. Finally, a little tinplate box sealed with wax is fastened to the top of his head, over his cap, which contains matches. Everything is placed up there that must not get wet. In addition, they each have a flask of eau-de-vie suspended from one hip, a spare pair of shoes suspended from the other, a good knife in the right-hand pocket and a pipe in the left.

At a few minutes to eleven, the door opens slightly; a slender shadow passes through first, belly down, then a larger one follows it. Those two strange animals crawl as far as the marsh, part the water-lentils gently, and, without any noise or any effort, let themselves slide slowly under the black plants. Two heads appear, mingled with the thick tufts of duckweed; those two heads have water up to the ears and are breathing through the nose. They are 377 and 378.

VII
How the Amour of Toads Can Influence Human Destinies, and the Inconvenience of Tinplate Matchboxes

THEY go on, with their feet in the mud, their bodies under water and their faces level with the weeds, feeling the pustules of a toad crushed against their cheek at every step. Around them, the flat leaves sink under the twisted bodies of enlaced couples, which are singing by inflating their throats.

Marius, more delicate and more nervous, suffers horribly from that repulsive contact, and it requires all his strength of character and all his energy to prevent him uttering an exclamation of disgust when his lips encounter at water level the simultaneously rough and slimy skin of the large marsh toads. Jean, stronger against those sensations, contents himself with blowing vigorously when one of the reptiles is within range, and thus knocking it into the water between two leaves.

At one moment, however, he had, if not fear and disgust, at least embarrassment. He had found a kind of hole in the mud and, after a false step, had got out of it with a long stride. As he finished it, he found himself suddenly surrounded by the filthy beasts, which were swarming around his head. It seemed to him that he was rolling in a bath of toads. He had, in fact, fallen upon an entire band, stuck together and coagulated, as those animals are at the moment of spawning. There was a thick, sticky, palpitating paste, which seemed to be made of a single mass, but in which feet and limbs were stirring, agitating and stretching.

Marius would not have been able to help crying out if he had been enveloped by that living jelly. Even Jean could not repress a movement of recoil and horror; but it was brief. He recovered his self-possession immediately, dug his knotty fingers into the packet of agglutinated flesh without hesitation, and tore the whole amorous band apart with a slow effort. Then, in the midst of bloody leaves and viscous corpses, Jean went through first and Marius followed him.

At that moment, the moon showed the end of its horn behind a cloud and illuminated the black and swarming surface of the marsh. By its light, Marius thought he saw a movement in the advanced guard-post that was overlooking the direction of the plain. He touched Jean's arm under water and, raising his mouth out of the water, whispered to him to look. In fact, the red dot of the lamp illuminating the guard-post had just shifted. It disappeared momentarily, and then reappeared at the door. Adjutant Barbellez was carrying it, and seemed to be indicating the marsh to his two companions. Jean and Marius were only two hundred paces away from the group.

This is what had happened.

In tearing apart the mass of toads Jean had not been able to avoid making a certain amount of noise. One of his hands had even landed flat on a nenuphar, with a sonorous click. Barbellez had keen ears, and the sound, propagated very well over the surface of the water, had reached him clearly through the open window. He had got up and looked out

"It isn't a toad that sings like that," he said. "That sound resembled a slap, or a misfired pistol shot. Hmm, that's odd!"

And he had come out with his two acolytes to see whether the three of them could discover anything.

In the midst of tufts of black weed and groups of toads, however, it was impossible to distinguish two human heads, especially covered by the dark woolen cap that is the headgear of deportees. That was confounded with the obscure and bumpy surface of the marsh. Thus, the three guards searched in vain with their gaze the whole extent of the marshy plain. They did not see anything. The two fugitives were no longer moving.

Barbellez was about to go back inside when he finally perceived something, a sort of pale reflection, as if there were a silver plaque on a leaf.

"What the devil is that?" he said to his men. "Look! There, at the tip of my finger. It's glinting in the moonlight. Do you see? One would think that it were moving. What can it be?"

It was the tinplate box that Marius had fixed on top of his cap. In spite of his firm desire to remain completely motionless, he had been unable to avoid moving his head to avoid a toad, and in the new position that he was occupying, the metal was reflecting the rays of moonlight.

"Damn!" whispered Jean Pioux. "Have they seen us, the beggars? They seem to be looking straight at us. Do you know if that damned Barbellez has good eyes?"

"Shut up and don't make so much noise," Marius replied. "They can't see us, I tell you."

Now, Barbellez could see the pale reflection of the box very clearly, but neither he nor the others could guess what it might be. They were no longer thinking about the noise of a little while before as something suspect, but they were intrigued by that piece of metal shining in the middle of the marsh.

"In truth," said Barbellez, "I want to have a clear heart. I'll find out what it is. My rifle, Brigadier. I'll fire a bullet at it by way of reconnaissance. It's only two hundred meters away, and I'll be damned if I can't hit the bull's eye of a target at two hundred meters! You'll see how one can smash a moonbeam with a rifle shot."

When he had his rifle, he stared at the white dot before taking aim.

"Damn!" said Jean to Marius, raising his mouth out of the water again. You can see that it's us that the swine's looking at, and he's going to send us a plum. We have to dive."

"Will you shut up, wretch! Dive? They'd be sure to hear us and see us. We'd be done for. Stay still."

"But they can see us, I tell you. Look—he's taking aim, He's going to fire. Should we dive?"

"Don't budge, damn it. We'll see what he can see, because he never misses, the old bastard. It isn't us he can see, for sure; we don't have anything visible.

He had not finished when he received seething like a slap on the head. At the same time, a metallic sound resonated in his ears. He thought he had been wounded, but did not say a word or make a movement. Jean had not moved either, but he immediately whispered in his ear: "It's the matchbox."

"Idiot that I am! That's true! Well, so much the better that he got it—now he can't see it any longer."

"He seems to be enjoying himself now!"

"Shh! Stay still. If he does it again, we're done for."

"Fortunately, he no longer has anything to aim at."

That was exactly what Barbelez was thinking. He had laughed at first, with contentment, and then laughed at the astonishment of his men, amazed by his skill. Then his curiosity returned.

"Well, we're no further forward, are we? I'm an imbecile. I amused myself like a child, firing a rifle shot, and we don't know at what."

"Bah!" said the brigadier. "It isn't always a man's eye. Anyway, it'd be a rude fellow who could take that shot without saying anything. Come on, Père Barbellez—there's still a drop of taiga in the bottom of the bottle."

"That's true. Let's go inside. There's nothing to be done. I'll have to go out in a boat tomorrow to see if any traces remain."

And they went back inside.

When everything had resumed its normal physiognomy and the door as closed, the interior light softened by the glass of the window and the silence of the night extended once again over the sleeping landscape, Marius risked moving, and said to Jean:

"Let's go, my friend; the hardest part is over. Forward ho!"

Half an hour after that terrible incident, they finally arrived at the mouth of the stream and went along it, still neck-deep in the water, under the somber dome of the mangroves.

IX
The Doorless Tomb

AS Marius had foreseen, it was even worse than in the marsh, if not for horror and danger, at least for difficulty.

The water was glacial. In order to warm up a little, they suspended themselves from time to time from the branches above their heads, pulling themselves up out of the water by the strength of their arms. They shook themselves for a moment in order to stimulate the circulation of the blood. There were, moreover, rather long stretches where, unable to find a foothold, even near the banks, which were sheer, they had to swim and thus make headway against a rapid current. When one swims for too long in water that is too cold, the limbs stiffen, grow weary and become heavy, and the muscles are soon twisted by cruel cramps that paralyze the strength and even stop all movement.

Jean succumbed to that first. The more nervous nature of Marius, who had not been able to overcome the disgust of the marsh, undoubtedly supported the cold better. Suddenly, Jean said to him: "Listen, old man, I can't do any more. It'll soon be six hours that we've been marching like this in this icy bath. It's worn me out. For more than a quarter of an hour I've had a terrible cramp in my right calf, and kept going anyway, but now I'm finished. Leave me here, old man, and head for the mountain on your own. It can't be very far. It'll soon be daylight; it's beginning to get brighter. If we both stay here you'll be caught. I'd rather be caught on my own. You need to find Jeanne. I'll tell the guards that you drowned. You hear, Marius?"

"Yes, I hear, but I don't understand. And it's an idiot who thinks that I can leave him here and save myself like a coward. No, no way, José. I listened to you spout your little tirade because it seemed so funny to hear such stupid things. Will you put a sock in it, you great canary! Let's go! Let's get out of this, damn it; we'll find a means of hiding in a tree until this evening, and continue during the night . . ."

"If nothing bad happens to us between now and then," Jean interjected.

As if he had made a prediction, he suddenly saw Marius, who was five or six paces ahead, plunge into the water and disappear as if into a hole.

The water was turbulent at the place where Marius had sunk, and by the vague daylight that was increasing, Jean saw that there was a kind of whirlpool there. That whirlpool was about to devour him too, if he did not get out as quickly as possible. No matter! His duty was to follow Marius, to save him if there was a means, or to die with him if death was at the bottom of that abyss.

Scarcely has he seen Marius plunge and the surface of the water seethe than Jean moves forward, bounding as much as the current permits, and in an instant he is at the place where his friend was a moment before. But he suddenly feels his leg, which he has extended forward as if to walk, seized, as if by a hand, and violently drawn. He loses his footing and is engulfed. He spins like a waltzer, or like a rapidly-plunging corkscrew.

There is a momentary pause; he puts a foot on the bottom but then he feels himself abruptly thrust back diagonally by a current of water much less cold than that of the stream, almost lukewarm. All that in one minute! Then he finds his head out of the water again, swimming in a mild and calm basin, but in profound obscurity, still carried by a kind of flux that is impelling him. He cannot see anything, does not know anything, does not understand anything, and can only hear a distant murmur of vague noises, doubtless the sound of the whirlpool that seized him and then let him go.

Where am I? he wonders *Where's Marius? Has he, like me, had the good fortune to encounter the benevolent current? Or has the whirlpool broken him against the bed? Poor Marius? But what am I going to do?*

Thinking and dreaming thus, he swam, still following the thread of the water, without taking account of his strange situation, nor becoming accustomed to the somber atmosphere that surrounds him, not having the presence of mind to do anything, even to cry out.

He was putting out his arms, therefore, slowly, making long strokes mechanically, when he felt something damp and silky beneath his fingers. He withdrew his hand rapidly, and then instinctively stuck it out again. It was a clump of hair.

He drew the object toward him almost effortlessly, because of the water in which it was bathed, but sensing perfectly that there as something heavy beneath the hair; it was a body.

While swimming, he lifted the body on to his shoulder, with the head out of the water. Obviously, it was Marius, but he was either dead or unconscious,

"Oh, damn!" exclaimed Jean Pioux. "If only I had a foothold, I could try to reanimate him. The poor fellow's drowned! Now my leg's getting numb again; the cramp is coming back."

And he thought: *Oh, this will never end, this subterranean river. Where's the bank, then? It's not a river, it's a lake. It can't go on forever, though. I'll go on to the end, and I'll let myself go down with him rather than let him go.*

And he kept going, exhausted, out of breath, swimming rapidly now, in order to arrive sooner, stiffening himself against his twisted muscles. He tried to cut through the current sideways, and thought that he might find a limit that way, a wall of rock or a sandbank—something, at any rate. Marius' heavy head was swinging against his own, but he was careful to place himself back-to-back with him, and the mouth of the drowned man, thus being in the air, was not exposed to ingurgitating any more water. With his left hand, Jean kept it fixed against his shoulder, and cut through the water forcefully with his right hand.

But the effort was too rude and too long, especially after the countless fatigues and the six hours of cold that he had suffered since the previous day. He sensed his vigor ebbing away, his body becoming heavier and heavier and his respiration more halting; his feet went numb, only reaching out weakly, and fell inert, vertical in the water, without touching bottom. He thought that he was doomed, caught between the alternatives of letting go of Marius and saving himself, thus lightened, or sinking with his friend. He did not hesitate.

"We're out of luck," he said, aloud. "It's necessary to die here. I'll let myself sink."

"What?" said Marius, in a faint voice.

And at the same time, as Jean already had water up to his lips, his feet encountered rock. He took a step forward. He touched bottom. They were saved.

He went forward. The water gradually let go. It was soon only up to his armpits. Another three steps and it rose no further than his breast. In one minute, his strength was multiplied tenfold by joy. He made four or five bounds in the darkness with his burden, blindly, imprudently, at the risk of breaking his head against a wall. But no! There was no wall, and he found himself on solid ground, with Marius, who was coming round.

"Marius, my old Marius, we're safe! We're no longer in the water. Look!"

But Marius, awake again, could not see anything, because they were still in the dark.

"Oh, how stupid I am," said Jean. "I forgot that there's no light. Anyway, you can feel the ground under your feet, can't you? We're safe, eh?"

"Where are we then? My head's heavy and my heart's upside down."

"Of course—you were drowned."

"Has the day finished, then? It was just beginning when we were separated."

"We're in a cave, my friend, I don't know where. But now I think of it, me who thought we were saved—how are we going to get out of here?"

"We'll see about that later. For the moment, let's have something to eat and get some sleep. No one's going to come to look for us in here."

Groping, they took a little bread out of their sacks. Although it was damp, they washed it down with a little eau-de-vie; then, in spite of the hardness of the rock and their wet clothes, they went to sleep, and even started snoring conscientiously.

When they woke up, it naturally seemed to them that they felt a little better. They broke another crust, and, sleep having replenished their strength, they felt restored.

"It's not everything," said Marius then, "to have slept, eaten and dried ourselves off a little. Now it's a matter of finding our route. That's not easy. We must be in some cavern without issues, for we can't see daylight anywhere. To retrace our steps isn't possible. Besides which, we don't need another bath; we were sufficiently cleaned up yesterday. So, nothing remains to us but to march with our backs turned to the lake. Let's go!"

They took a few steps, holding one another by the hand, and arrived thus at the water's edge, which wet their feet.

"Necessary not to do that, old dear," growled Jean, with a coarse laugh. "I've just got out of that, thanks! We'll bid you adieu!"

"But not that it'll be a pleasure to see you again," added Marius.

And, turning around, they plunged boldly into the black void that opened in front of them. The air there was cool because of the lake, but heavy and stifling because of the stagnation that it experienced in the cave. One might have thought it the warm, damp atmosphere of an oven that had been washed. Pebbles rolled under their feet and sand was crushed. Above them there was doubtless a high vault, for the echo of their footsteps and their voices resonated there strongly. Where did it end?

For more than half an hour they walked like that—slowly, to be sure, as one walks in darkness, but advancing nevertheless, without finding any end to their journey. They were still hopeful.

"Damn Barbellez!" said Marius. "If that swine hadn't sent my box of matches to kingdom come, we'd at least be able to see something."

"Aha!" Jean replied. "I've just felt something brush my head, like a branch. Perhaps there are plants suspended from the vault. We're doubtless getting to the end."

Soon, in fact, they reached a wall of sorts, covered with sharp asperities, and harder than the rock.

"Pay attention!" said Marius. "It's necessary to follow it, feeling our way. It will take us somewhere."

Another half an hour of marching! They went more rapidly; the wall served them as a rail and a guide. Jean was in front and increasing his pace even further when he suddenly cried: "Devil take this wall! We've come back to the lake. That's amusing!"

"Let's turn round," replied Marius. "We'll follow the same system. At least we'll have made a tour of our prison and put a hand on all the walls."

Another hour of traveling, their fingers feeling the wall, their feet indecisive, their eyes wide open in the darkness, with hope and anxiety in their hearts. Would they find a fissure?

They found the water again. They had traveled the entire circumference that formed the back of the myste-rious cavern. Facing them was the water, with no other outlet than the gulf from which the current emerged and into which, consequently, they could not plunge even if they could find it again. Behind them was the darkness, a prison, death from starvation, with no possibility of rescue for which to wait. They did not even have the courage any longer to eat.

They both had the same idea: "It's better to kill ourselves."

What a destiny! Born on the luminous pavements of Paris, brought up in the sunlight, growing up in the open air, it was necessary for them, then, to croak in this darkness, to be buried alive in this asphyxiation.

A sob rose to Marius' lips; he threw himself into Jean's arms.

It was only a momentary discouragement, for he immediately started laughing, saying: "Bah! What do you want to do?"

"I want . . . I want to finish it right away, of course," replied Jean.

"Come on, don't say that in such a lugubrious tone! I want to finish it too, and it won't take long, will it? Two ticks and three movements. But that's no reason to be sad. What's the point of weeping like a sponge, or making a deep voice, like an ophicleide? What the hell! We were born joyful, we've lived cheerfully, it's necessary to die laughing. For myself, I think we've still been lucky."

"Lucky!"

"Of course! We could have been eaten, couldn't we? Roasted on a spit?"

"Well, it's no more amusing being here, cooked in an oven."

"Pooh! Personally, I prefer the oven, and then, the spit or the oven, what does it matter? It's necessary to look away, that's all I can see. There's only one thing that consoles me. We decamped in order to be free. Well, we are! Hurrah for liberty!"

In spite of that cheerful attitude, they remained silent for a long moment.

Then, suddenly, an immense din shook the vault.

X

Which concerns Coral and Volcanic Islands, and a few Religious Rites

NEW CALEDONIA offers the curious phenomenon of being both a coral and a volcanic island.[1]

Everyone knows what a coral island is; a reef of coral, an immense edifice built by microscopic laborers, gradually rises up, by virtue of an insensible but irresistible effort, stopping in its crevices everything that passes by, everything that floats, marine moss with long curly hair, algae similar to dark green leather straps, shingle polished by the perpetual gentle friction of the waves, empty seashells that crumble gradually, like houses falling into ruins, all the thousand kinds of debris, all the nameless and countless things that form the bottomless mud of the sea, sand and slime, an enormous mass that a typhoon sometimes comes to wake from its slumber, tear from its bed, and which then rolls in the eddies of the waves, as dust rises in whirlwinds in a storm wind. With all that substance retained in passing, the coral reef covers itself, fills itself and blocks its holes. And thus an island forms, which has the coral for

---

1 This is not true; New Caledonia is neither a coral island nor a volcanic island. The account of the Kanak inhabitants of the island is also completely fanciful.

a carcass, and for flesh the thick, soft lees that float in the great cup of the sea.

A volcanic island is not made slowly like that. It is born suddenly, a daughter of fire. The interior lava finds itself too narrowly confined, it swells with its vapor the solid crust that serves as a lid for the vase in which it is contained, and that lid, which is the seabed, forms a mountain that surpasses the surface. There it bursts in a volcano, or the entire mass of fire solidifies in granite. Hence, an island.

Now, it often happens that on that crust of earth swollen by the volcano, there is an entire population of madrepores. And thus that coral reef, built in order to arrive at the surface of the water, is carried up in the air like a hill. The reefs become rocks.

From that emerges a singular phenomenon. In places, in the elevated mountain, interior collapses occur, collapses of all the soft part, which have only left in the air the skeleton of the soil, and which thus, in the coral island, lay bare in the heart of the mountain, far from the sea, coral caverns.

Some are closed to the light in all places; they only open to watercourses that flow and are engulfed in darkness, or subterranean tunnels that come to emerge there after having crawled through darkness for a long time.

It is in a cavern of that sort that Jean and Marius found themselves.

Only, by feeling the wall, they had not been able to discover any issue, the only issue from the cavern not being at floor level. It was a big hole in the depths of that wall, but toward the middle of its height, about fifteen feet from the base. To those who arrived there in the dark, it gave the impression of a mouth open to the void.

That mouth is, for the savages, the door to a temple.
The mysterious grotto, with its funereal lake, is, in their
superstition, the horrible and sacred dwelling of the ancestors. Every year, the sorcerers and the chiefs come in order
to accomplish religious ceremonies there.

They enter the subterrain, and they crawl there for half
a league, silently, in the dark, in single file, face down.

It is the oldest sorcerer who is in the lead, and who
regulates that slow procession with his footfalls.

When he arrives at the orifice that overlooks the grotto,
the rocky edge of which he senses under his fingers, he
stops. The entire file gathers behind him and everyone
stops in his turn. Then, abruptly, they all stand up and
utter a savage cry.

It is that cry that Jean and Marius have just heard.

A new sound reached them thereafter, like an animal
leaping to the ground from above. It was repeated three
times; then there was something like the rustle of a body
sliding against something. Then the jumps resumed, fre-
quent and regular. Then there was a cry; all that done in
the most profound silence.

That was the band of sorcerers and chiefs penetrating
into the grotto. Three chiefs, the youngest, had jumped
first. Then they had put their backs to the wall; the first
had climbed up on to the shoulders of the second and that
one on the third, in such a fashion as to form a human
ladder up to the tunnel entrance. By those steps, made
of arms, torsos and legs, the sorcerers had let themselves
slide down, their religious character conferring on them
the right to descend thus, along with the old chiefs, whose
age merits that honor. Then the crowd had jumped, and
they had all arranged themselves one by one along the wall,
without saying a word.

The old priest who leads the solemnity must not come down until the end. In order to begin the ceremony he remains on the edge of the subterrain, from which he pronounces the sacred formulae and the prayers. It is only on his order, and after the customary incantations, that torches are lighted, the rank is broken and everyone goes to dip his new amulets in the mysterious water of the lake.

Before commencing, everyone else being down below and the old priest up above, everyone has to meditate and say in the secrecy of his heart the prayer that he has come to address to the ancestors.

During that moment of silence, Jean and Marius had advanced quietly behind a rock that they felt beneath their hands. When their first emotion had passed, they now had to consult one another about what it was necessary to do in the presence of that unknown danger. They whispered into one another's ears.

"What can that be?" said Jean.

"In truth, I don't know," Marius replied. "They're not animals, for sure. Animals make more noise than that, and wouldn't have uttered that isolated cry, which can only have come from human throats, and resembles a war cry. Perhaps they're savages. I've sometimes heard mention of their religious ceremonies. This must be something of that sort. Anyway, we're going to see."

XI
Which Describes the Marvelous Grotto Marvelously

INDEED they were.

The old priest had uttered a shrill cry, and immediately, almost simultaneously, a row of sparks had appeared at the back of the cave, like as many abruptly opening eyes.

They were the savages' flints, which were igniting their resin torches.

When the torches were lit, Jean and Marius were dazzled.

That cavern is about a thousand meters in diameter and twenty-five or thirty high. It is bordered by a wall that rises vertically at first, for nearly ten meters, and then begins to curve in a spherical cap. But what renders that wall strange and splendid is that it is made of coral.

The straight part, doubtless formed from the foundations of the madreporic edifice, is accumulated in a dense mass. The ceiling, by contrast, is very uneven, very jagged, bristling with red branches twisted in all directions, sticking out, turning back on themselves, turning abruptly one way or another, stalactites in the form of lightning bolts, inextricable bundles of bizarrely entangled bloody zigzags. Each branch is covered with a thousand little black holes made by the sand deposited therein. That stands out against the red background like an embroidery in festoons with imperceptible tips.

The yellow light of the torches tries in vain to penetrate that brushwood. It breaks up therein and is scattered in the fissures, and the radiance glinting on the ridge of an angle makes the retreat behind it seem darker. The vacillating flame and the thick smoke of the resin, the cloud of which flows, give fantastic appearances to that prodigious sculpture. It resembles the swarming of I know not what venomous beasts, struggling and mingling in knots with red serpents.

Here and there, a plant hangs down. Sometimes it is an ancient, desiccated, stiff alga. One might think it a flamboyant blade traversing that white heap of twisted reptiles. Sometimes it is a liana, long and supple, with thin lacy leaves, which trembles at every flexion of the fiber like the multitudinous feet of an agonizing centipede.

Red and somber under the yellow light or the black smoke, with flashes and dark holes, all of that is swarming, enlacing, knotting, tearing and biting; and the vision is so alive that, in spite of the silence that sleeps in the grotto, one thinks one can hear, up above, all the rumor of a monstrous battle: shrill hissing, the friction of crawling bodies, muffled growls, sharp grating sounds, the slithering of crawling bodies, the crack of tightening coils and the viscous ripping of skin from which blood is spurting, and into which spines are plunging, which break there with a dry click.

The ground offers a less fantastic aspect, but perhaps even more splendid, than the ceiling. Scattered there, fallen in the disorder of collapse, are all the minerals and stones forming the body of the mountain. Marble with sharp ridges is dressed in all colors there, from white to somber black. Pink blocks resemble petrified flowers. Others are a tender green, like the first shoots of April, and their hue is combined with those of schorl, which is a bright green,[1] jasper, which is a dark green, and nephrite, which has black veins. Quartz crystals scintillate everywhere, transparent and clear. Some, opaque and milky, have the appearance of tarnished mirrors. Gray slate with white reflections is sown here and there in blocks whose edges are crumbling, like fringes. In places, silvery plaques lie dormant like pools of water in moonlight. That is black coal, which has an ebony sheen, talc, the silvery leaves of which resemble the scales of some enormous fish.

The ground itself, a carpet on which all these gleams are laid out, is not like ordinary earth, brown and dull. It is greasy and shiny clay, saturated with iron oxide, which makes it ocher red.

Thus, one thinks one is seeing a gigantic sculpted mosaic, all of whose scintillating fragments are framed in a paste made of petrified coral, or powdered blood.

The mosaic stops abruptly toward the middle of the grotto, as if it were cut by a great glass blade. That glass blade is the water. Its regular current follows the edge with the monotony of an unrolled ribbon. It shines with an insensible movement. Further away, it plunges into a profound darkness where the eye can only see emptiness, from which a slow breeze comes that seems to have weighted down its wings by brushing a sheet of oil.

---

1 Actually schorl is a brown or black variety of tourmaline.

XII
In which Tattoos are Ridiculed,
Thanks to Taboo

HUDDLED behind their rock, Marius and Jean were stupefied by that strangely beautiful spectacle.

Once their torches were lit, the savages had resumed their silent pose.

A shrill and rapid hum, which suddenly rose up, extracted the two friends from their ecstasy. It was the old priest, who was commencing the incantations.

Marius risked a peep and, leaning out of his hiding place slightly, was able to see the curious ceremony.

About thirty savages were aligned along the wall, each one carrying a smoky torch at the end of his extended right arm. Given the rigidity of their stance, the yellow or brown color of their bodies and the immobility with which they were holding the torches, one might have thought them a row of bronze torch-brackets.

They were coiffed in accordance with the rites of great festivals—which is to say that the hair was gathered in a tuft at the summit of the cranium, heightened by a feather and reddened with chalk. That made a sort of bizarre helmet that seemed to be resting on the ears, large and protruding, open like a fan, the lobes pierced with enormous holes.

Their only vestments were amulets, green serpentine necklaces, bracelets of nacreous seashells, a loincloth and russet fur anklets. Their true costume was tattooing: not tattoos resembling brushwork, as among the redskins of America, but tattoos in relief. Such tattoos are produced by moxas made with twigs of resinous plants, which are stuck in the skin and set alight in the puncture. The moxas, being disposed with a certain symmetry, leave scars on the form of ampoules, which make the goffered skin resemble the pustulous hide of a toad.

Even more profoundly tattooed, and more extensively covered with necklaces, bracelets and, above all, amulets, are the sorcerers. Almost all of them are infirm, lame or one-armed, hump-backed or legless. Their distinctive ornament is a bonnet of black felt, tall and pointed, like that of the magicians of our tales; its hair is rough and the extremely terminated in a wisp.

The sorcerers were not holding torches and were not lined up like the chiefs. They were crouching in a group directly beneath the tunnel, at the orifice of which the high priest was standing. The latter wore a bonnet taller than all the rest. His white beard was braided into a large mat, which descended to his loincloth. He was holding both arms aloft—arms terminated by crippled hands, a stump to the left and six splayed fingers to the right.

In a monotonous and high-pitched voice, he spoke with an extraordinary volubility. At times when he disappeared in the smoke of the torches, Marius, unable to see him, was put in mind of exceedingly dry vine-branches twisting in the depths of ovens with a rapid and staccato crackle.

The prayer went on for a long time. Marius had time to see clearly, to understand what he was seeing, and to

reflect. The religious and sacred character of the ceremony
was evident. It was therefore necessary either to take advantage of it or become its victim, or to decide to remain
in hiding.

"Let's see, Jean—what are we going to do, old man?"

"Hmm. That's embarrassing. First it's necessary to know,
whatever we do, what they'll do. If we show ourselves, we're
cooked, aren't we—cooked being the right word—roasted
like chickens, eh?"

"That's possible. But if we don't show ourselves, we're
buried, that's for sure. We can't get out of here. To hope to
climb as far as that hole, whatever your strength and my
skill might be, is folly. Would you rather we stay here?"

"No, of course not. What are we going to do, then?"

"Listen. I have an idea. I've been ruminating it for a
while. They're in the process of praying, aren't they? To
whom? It's all the same to me: God, the Devil, their ancestors, ghosts, it doesn't matter. What's certain is that
this place is sacred to them, that they come here with a
religious terror and won't be astonished to see something
supernatural here. You follow my reasoning?"

"Yes, yes, I see what you're getting at. You want us to
pass ourselves off as good gods, and you think they'll swallow it. Good gods in clothes! Good gods with caps! It won't
work, I tell you."

"Listen, then, damn it. It's all a matter of preparation.
And then, what tells you that I want to appear before them
fully dressed? They're putting themselves before us naked;
I don't see why I should put on gloves with them and why
I should be obstinate in keeping my trousers on when they
only have fig leaves."

"Oh, you make me laugh!"

"Do you want us to stay behind our rock like lice on a comb, or will you follow my idea, take the risk and try to get out of here?"

"Go for your idea—it's the lesser of two evils. And at least it will be funny. We'll amuse ourselves a little."

"Good, it's settled. Let's begin, then. Let's undress without making a noise, and leave the rest to me."

In a matter of moments they were as naked as worms. Jean's powerful back and broad chest quivered in the darkness, while Marius shrank his supple spine and pulled his long neck into his shoulders.

The old priest's rapid prayer was still continuing.

"Damn!" said Jean. "Is he ever going to finish with his chattering? He's going to take our skin for a sign!"

The old man finished at that moment, in a very shrill tone, and he was about to say the final formula, the formula of taboo. "Taboo" is the label applied indifferently to the consecration of a thing or a person, and the thing or person consecrated. Everything that is taboo is inviolable, under penalty of sacrilege.

The old man then sang, in a slow voice, like a grave chant, the following hymn:

> *Taboo! Taboo! Taboo!*
> *Taboo is the spirit of the ancestors with the high hair, the holed ears and the tattooed breast! Taboo are those who have quit the vale of hunger, and who have departed for the blue land, where the air is tobacco smoke and the soul is the flower of yams. They spend the day killing fat prisoners, whose flesh they roast. They spend the night strolling in perfumed arbors with lovely*

women with shaven heads painted white, with long pear-shaped breasts.

Taboo! Taboo! Taboo!

Taboo are those who have dipped their amulet in the black lake where the ancestors washed their bodies before the great voyage! Taboo are they, for they will always have their pipe studded and their ladle full. They will sell their daughters dearly to young men thirsty for Virgin Water. They will drink the blood of the vanquished and the milk of captives. And when the day of the great storm comes, they will have a cabin ready on the mountain, a very safe cabin, such that, if the snow falls, the snow will not soak it, but will make it a mantle of cotton; such that, if the hail falls, the hailstones will be encrusted in the roof like diamonds and make it resemble a sky studded with stars.

Taboo! Taboo! Taboo!

Taboo is everything that sleeps in this grotto, everything that floats in the lake, the animals and the things, the spirits of the ancestors and the bodies of the living.

Taboo! Taboo! Taboo!

He finished in a loud voice, and the echoes responded, melancholy and profound, as if they were dragging the sounds over the lugubrious water of the lake.

But now, the noise of the echoes having concluded, a new and distant voice rose up and, in a more muted tone, repeated three times, quite distinctly:

"Taboo! Taboo! Taboo!"

The old priest was stupefied, and the chiefs, forgetting the sacred order of the rite, drew closer to the group of sorcerers, who had suddenly stood up, in disorder. No one dared to say a word. All of them were trembling. They were waiting to see what the man who had talked to the spirits was going to do and to order.

He was lying prone on the ground, his head protruding over the edge of the tunnel. He muttered a few shreds of prayers, agitating his lips as much as possible. His long, braided beard followed the rapid movement of his chin, reminiscent of a white fish prey to the feverish convulsions of death.

All gazes were turned toward him. But instead of taking courage, they could only be more frightened on seeing that distraught face, and those haggard and wide-open eyes; they thought they were seeing a severed head, ready to fall into the grotto, retained on the edge of the tunnel by some claw that was shaking it.

Finally, the old priest recovered his senses; and, getting up on to his knees, he extended his arms once again toward the cavern, saying: "Taboo is you, spirit who talks to us! What do you want, memory of the ancestors who has remained in this grotto as the sound of the waves remains in the depths of seashells?"

A new voice, closer and in a higher register, immediately replied: "Taboo! Taboo! Taboo!"

Then, without the savages having had time to get over their fright, while all of them, imitating the old priest, had thrown themselves face down on the ground, yet another voice was heard, then a third and then a new one, and then an infinite number of voices. And all those different voices spoke from all points of the grotto, saying, crying,

howling and moaning by turns the same word: "Taboo . . . !
Taboo . . . ! Taboo . . . !"

There were muffled and profound words that seemed
to come from the utmost depths of the darkness, where
the vague waves were splashing. Others fell from the vault,
jerkily, as if ripped by the coral branches. Sometimes they
yelped like barking dogs and came closer, so to speak,
crawling. They often burst forth in the very midst of the
savages, who huddled together and climbed on top of one
another then, like frightened sheep. Each of them thought
that he had heard his neighbor cry out.

Already, the most frightened were beginning to stand
up against the wall, preparing to flee, without caring
any longer about the ceremony or the old priest whose
head was bobbing madly up above, eyelids closed and lip
sagging.

Suddenly, the cries ceased.

Timidly, the old sorcerer opened his eyes. The chiefs
who were about to climb up fell face down again. All heads
were raised, like the heads of dogs on the alert. They dared
to look into the shadow.

Horror! They saw a bizarre being becoming detached
from the wall, emerging from behind a rock, which began
to grow, until they were able to distinguish a kind of human being formed by two naked bodies, which linked two
heads posed one on top of the other, in such a fashion that
the animal had two legs down below, which were walking,
and two grimacing faces in the middle, framed by four
arms holding hands and another two legs at the top, agitating in all directions in a menacing fashion

It was Jean Pioux the Hercules, carrying Marius
Mazuclard the ventriloquist balanced on his head.

XIII
How Priests Make Miracles

SORCERERS and priests are the same everywhere, far less religious than political.

The old leader of the ceremony, who had been afraid at first, quickly perceived the truth. He understood that the monster was simply formed of two men in an artificial posture, and he did not require a great effort of reasoning to divine that the two men in question had doubtless escaped from the prison camp. He only needed to say a few words to enlighten his ignorant companions, and, religious terror being vanquished by priestly authority, the so-called monster would be torn apart.

But the old priest preferred to take advantage of the miracle. He already enjoyed a great influence over several tribes, because he was reputed to converse mentally with the spirits. What would his power not be if he were seen in commerce with them? He would become more than a priest, almost a supernatural being himself. From then on, he would be able to bend the will of the chiefs to his own, to recommence, with the support of the people, the famous Conspiracy of Spirits and reestablish the government of the ancestors, a sort of theocratic monarchy of which he would be the pontiff-king.

That reasoning passed through his mind like a vision. At the same time, he let himself slide down along the three young chiefs who were serving as a ladder. Once on the ground he uttered a shrill cry; then, his infirm hand having commanded everyone to be silent, he advanced toward the apparition alone.

All the prostrated savages were paralyzed by fright. The breath could be heard panting in their breasts and whistling in their throats. Teeth were chattering as in the grip of winter under the snow. Only a few sorcerers, long-time confidants of their old chief, suspected a pious deceit. But they only fostered more terror in order to assist the religious effect that it was necessary to produce.

Meanwhile, Jean and Marius continued walking slowly, wanting by means of a long apparition to overexcite the imagination of the savages and prepare them for the ultimate presentation.

They were able to talk to one another in whispers, their two heads being juxtaposed.

"Are they foolish enough?" sniggered Marius. "There they all are, as flat as soles."

"In truth, I wouldn't have thought it was so easy to pass for good gods. That's what they believe, evidently."

"That proves that they're good fellows."

Their cheerfulness was confused by the descent of the old man. They saw him advancing toward them, in such a resolute manner that they dreaded something.

"Well," said Jean, slowing down, "that one doesn't give the impression of having bought it."

"So it seems to me. But how can that be? He was so frightened a moment ago."

"Damn! He's one who can see clearly, that's all. He was frightened by the ventriloquism. That's understandable; ventriloquism is a true phenomenon. But now he doesn't want to let himself be played for a fool. He can see perfectly well that our phenomenon is fake, like a monster in costume."

"Oh, you're chattering like a one-eyed magpie, my old Jean, instead of reflecting on what we ought to do."

"What we ought to do? I can only see one thing. If the old man comes right up to us, you let go of one of my hands, ensure your equilibrium and I'll knock the fellow out with a punch. Is that a good plan?"

"Yes, I can't see another, either. And what's excellent about that plan is that the others will be even more frightened, and we'll be able to do whatever we want with them. Go for the punch!"

But the old man did not come right up to them. He stopped some ten paces away; and, as they were still advancing, he said to them, in a low voice and in bad French: "Friend of you. Good *oui ouis* and good priest do together. Good priest old. Do no harm to you. Nor you to him. Friend of you."

"Friend of you," replied Marius, as Jean came to a halt.

The old man then advanced, crawling, in order to make the savages believe that he was worshiping the Spirit. When he was very close, he made a sign to the two friends to go back with him behind their rock, where they could reach an understanding more easily. And thus, him flat on the ground and them moving backwards with bizarre gestures, they gave the impression of vanishing into the wall.

There, everything was explained on either side. The old man revealed his projects. Jean and Marius admitted that they had escaped from Port-de-Prince. The old man set out his qualities as a sorcerer, priest and physician. The acrobats spoke about the innumerable tricks they could perform. They understood one another. They saw that the three of them could forge a very powerful alliance.

They had, therefore, a service to render one another mutually. The old man told them that Jeanne was indeed a prisoner of the indigenes, and promised to take them to her. They promised in return to lend themselves to his religious mummeries.

One sole point was subject to negotiation: that was to determine who would render the first service.

"Give us the captive," said Marius, "And afterwards, we'll do whatever you want."

"No," said the priest. "First, do everything I want, and I'll repay you by giving you the captive." He added the very just reasoning that, the greater his influence was, the easier it would be for him to satisfy his friends. The young woman was in the power of a powerful chief who wanted to make her his wife. In order to struggle with him, the old man needed to augment his prestige. Thus, in serving him, the two acrobats would be serving themselves.

But Marius did not want to yield, dreading that he might be deceived by that bizarre ally. He consented to aid the old man immediately to strike a great blow by making a fine miracle, but on condition that the young woman should be brought to him the following day. From that moment on the two friends would lend themselves to all plans in order to bring the priest's conspiracy to a conclusion. When the *coup d'état* was terminated, if the old sorcerer was victorious, he would give them the means to reach the nearest island inhabited by Europeans.

That conference had already lasted a long time, but the old man did not fear the impatience of the savages, toward whom, from time to time, he launched a fragment of prayer in order to let them know that he was still there.

He prolonged his absence further, in order to prepare the miracle. In fact, Jean and Marius had too European a nudity for spirits. The old man took stock. Many families had confided amulets to him in order that he might dip them in the lake personally. He covered his two aides with them, passing them around their necks, legs and wrists; then, mixing a little red ocher with saliva in the palm of his hand, he smeared their faces and bodies.

When everything was ready, all three of them emerged from their hiding place, uttering a loud cry, and they commenced the miracle.

Marius was standing on Jean's shoulders, and carrying the old priest himself in his two arms, raised in the air.

When the savages perceived that strange group in the distance, they recoiled in fear at first, crawling like dogs about to be beaten. They imagined that the monster had taken possession of the old man and was about to kill him or torture him in front of them. Tightly bunched together in an agitated heap, they did not dare either to go to his aid or run away. The majority muttered prayers without comprehending them, as rapidly as possible, in the hope making up for quality with quantity. A few, with more common sense, mentally offered the old priest in sacrifice to appease the Spirit. All of them, like animals that believe that they can avoid danger by refusing to see it, had closed their eyes.

The old priest sensed the full advantage of his position. Terrified as they were, the savages were his; he only had to maintain them in that state of excitement. From the height of his singular pulpit, formed by Jean and Marius, he started to say a short prayer, and imposed silence on them. Then he improvised the following hymn in a solemn voice and in a tone of mystical enthusiasm:

I have tamed the Spirit. I have beaten its strength. I have straddled its malice. I have my feet on its back.

In the water of the marsh, under the red sun and the white moon, by the winds from the north and the south, I have boiled the sacred herbs, the herbs that sweat, the flowers that stink.

I have mingled the green juice that makes yellow plaques on the skin, the blue juice that punctures the flesh and the black juice that eats away the bones.

I have eaten the head of the gecko, crushing it in my mouth.

I have rubbed my body with the bark of the manchineel that paralyzes.

I have washed my face with the sap of the Moluccan tree that blinds.

I have drunk the poisoned beverage, the beverage composed in accordance with the magical rite, the beverage made with herbs, plants and flowers, the green juice, the blue juice and the black juice, the beverage that kills and vivifies.

I have slept and I have awoken.

And I was dead and here I am, alive.

I have tamed the Spirit, I have beaten its strength, I have straddled its malice, I have my feet on its back!

The savages had raised their heads. Fear had given way to curiosity and admiration.

"Let the men gaze!" said the sorcerer. "Let them contemplate the Spirit, and venerate its tamer!"

At that moment, Marius descended from Jean's shoulders and placed the orator on the ground.

"Lelei! Lelei!" cried the old man. "Behold, the Spirit is divided in two. This is the Strength. And this is the Malice."

He indicated Jean, and then Marius.

"The priest is sacred!" he continued. "The sorcerer is holy! The art is omnipotent. I shall deliver myself to the games of the Spirit that is my slave."

And they commenced a series of tricks agreed in advance. It was understood between them that the old man would allow himself to be moved, handled and thrown, not opposing it in any way not being astonished by anything. As he was light because of his thinness and the body parts he lacked, Jean, and even Marius, could make use of him as an instrument and enable him to execute prodigies.

First Jean grasped him by the beard and lifted him up with one arm. In his large hand, and fingers as strong as a vice, the old man's head came to rest after describing a semicircle in space; and the sorcerer stayed thus for a moment, balanced head down at the end of that enormous arm, which resembled a stake traversing his body.

At the same time, Marius had coiled himself like a snake around the torso of the Hercules, and gradually climbed in a spiral toward the sorcerer's head. In that position they looked at one another, and all three began to sing, each to a different tune. The sorcerer intoned some incantation,

Jean uttered three notes as monotonous as an Angelus bell and Marius simply sang a Tyrolean ditty.

That made the most grotesque racket. Certainly, any other audience than that band of superstitious savages would have plugged their ears. People would have burst out laughing on hearing that precipitate quacking and low-pitched growling, festooned with the most implausible yodeling.

"I must say," said Jean Pioux to Marius, interrupting his throaty sounds, "that I've had enough. If this goes on the fellow will have a hemorrhage and I'm getting pins and needles in my arm. Let's go on to another exercise."

And while Marius loosened the coils of his twisted body, the Hercules swung the old man and deposited him on the ground, holding the summit of his cranium delicately between his thumb and index finger.

"Poor old chap," he said to him, jokingly, "you don't suspect that I've just performed with your carcass one of the best tricks in the world. Damn! That was nearly a hundred pounds that I held there for a moment *in a pinch*."

At that moment, Marius laughed as if to split his sides on examining the frightened expressions of the savages.

"Look how they're rolling big white eyes Jean!" he said. "One might think those eyes were trying to emerge from the heads in order to see more clearly."

As he finished laughing, he abruptly drew himself up to his full height, as he had the habit of doing in the public squares in order to commence his patter; and he unleashed that patter with an extraordinary volubility, without counting the phrases, with the particular tone of clowns, charlatans, parrots and hawkers in bazaars.

"Look, Messieurs, we haven't come here, my colleague and I, to offer you flea powder, tooth powder or horn powder. Flea powder's of little importance to you, since suicide is a crime, as the great philosopher Jean-Jacques, my pupil, has demonstrated. Horns are a superfluity that you don't know, having no shoes. And in any case, if you did know them, the powder would be quite useless to you. Horns are like the gods—they're eternal. There are only two fashions of treating them: when they're doing no harm, grab them by the waist, since they're *cors sages*; when they're inveterate, cover them with tar, because they're *cors d'age*. As for your teeth, Messieurs, you're too prudent and too ardent for me to give you the inside dope as regards teeth. I'll wash them for you, but for that, I'll use my saliva, and you can see that it's well prepared. No, Messieurs no, since again, I don't want to deceive you, my colleague and I are simple Hercules and acrobats. We've obtained the approval of several emperors, potentates, princes and others, and even Monsieur le Maire. And we're going to continue and vary the performance with a new, extraordinary feat that has never been done before, nor heard of, nor seen nor known, and I'm misleading you to prove that we're engaged, my colleague and I . . ."

"Haven't you finished rabbiting?" Jean Pioux interjected. "What a chatterbox!"

"On with the music, then!" said Marius.

At the same time, he stuck himself against Jean, threw himself in all fours, and assumed, as much as possible, the form of a barrel-organ, of which his forearm represented the handle. Jean lifted the old man up, sat him on his shoulders, and then clutched Marius' arms and caused it to pivot around its shoulder.

The organ started to play.

The astonishment of the savages immediately reached its peak. What they had considered so far was not so much the *tours de force* in themselves, but the power of the sorcerer who commanded them. Now, they admired above all the Spirit.

There was, in fact, something magical and supernatural about the spectacle.

A being, having human form, had gathered himself, shrunk himself and dislocated his body in such a fashion as to appear half as small, his thighs forming a sort of crush with his torso and his legs. He let his left arm go forth at hazard, in any direction, an inert thing that could be turned without releasing it from its socket and returned without breaking. The other arm was doubtless holding him suspended over Jean's abdomen, with a torsion of the foot between the Hercules' knees, his head, his neck, his will power—with everything and nothing, who knows?

And from that sunken chest, bruised by the drawn-back bones and striped by taut muscles, that disarticulated body in an impossible equilibrium, music emerged. It seemed that one ought to have heard frightful cries and horrible sounds departing from that tortured machine. One expected the grinding of teeth, the ripping of tendons, the muted fracturing of vertebrae and the snapping of bones breaking like glass. Instead, one heard an agreeable melody, accompanied by a bass always in harmony.

Jean provided the bass, with that voice simultaneously rumbling and piercing, which adopted for the key of F the mouth of a rheumatic bassoon.

Marius provided the song; a long time ago he had acquired an inimitable talent for imitating a barrel-organ.

He was able to give his larynx the palpitating sonorities of wooden pipes, or the tearful, tremulous whining sound, and suddenly release a long trill, like a fly beating its wings in a full nose and then flying away in a streak toward the blue sky. He knew the art of punctuating the notes with brief little pauses, fringing them, so to speak, putting hiccups of air between them, as the breathless voices of old sobbing organs do. He had all the faults, all the tears, all the sorrows of those wretched and sweet instruments, which give the most cheerful tunes I know not what heart-rending and melancholy charm.

The savages were touched, as all naïve people are by simple music. Their terror gradually relaxed into a less poignant emotion. They got up slowly from their flattened postures, sat on their heels, and let themselves go with the enervating flow of the melody. Tranquil and good tears ran down their smiling faces. At times, when a sharper note had a more penetrating tone, a quiver passed through all the bodies, which vibrated like strings caressed by a bow.

The effect was that which a pass produces on a magnetized subject, or a touch on a convulsive. The savages, swooning, were at Marius' discretion—which is to say, at the discretion of the Spirit; which is to say, again, that of the old priest who was commanding the Spirit.

The old man judged that it was necessary to leave it there for this time. At a word from him, Marius fell silent and Jean returned behind the rock with his double burden. The barrel organ became a man again, extended his limbs, put his ribs back in place and his bones in their sockets. The old man thanked them, bargaining as best he could. It was agreed that the two men would not leave the grotto, where they were perfectly safe. The old man would leave them flints and torches, and bring them food supplies in a few hours. At the same time he would give them news of Jeanne, whom he promised to bring within a day, no matter what the cost.

That said, he asked Marius to say a few words as before, very quickly and in a bizarre voice. Thus the Spirit would give them the impression of blessing him as he left the sanctuary.

And he returned to his companions, whom he had file out in silence, while Jean and Marius sang, like mirlitons, a scrap of a song by way of a benediction and a prayer:

"Oh, I've seen, I've seen!"
"Comrade, what have you seen?"
"I've seen a huge Hare
"Trembling with fever
"Under a bush."
"Comrade, you're right."

"Oh, I've seen, I've seen!"
"Comrade, what have you seen?"
"I've seen a cow
"Slip on the ice
"In the heart of summer."
"Comrade, you're lying."

As the last savage left, Marius hurled at him, puffing with laughter, this ludicrous adieu, a grotesque refrain that he had once sung to his bladder violin:

Mistico!
Dare dare, lire lire!
Clic! Clac! Clac!
Larouri laroura!
Tarantouru, Tatanturaire!
Saperlipopo!
Ricambo!
Saperlipopopiperlipopiperlipopette!
If you catch my drift,
You're very clever!

XIV
Betrothal

THE next day, faithful to his word, the old priest bought Jeanne, who threw herself like a madwoman into the arms of her two friends. And yet, in spite of their joy, the two friends had an almost embarrassed attitude in finding her again.

Jeanne was stark naked.

She only thought about that after the first impulse had passed, and started to blush, become anxious, and lowered her gaze. She did not know what to do. Jean and Marius no longer dared to look at her. It was both comical and charming.

Finally, they both had the same idea, and threw her their jackets, with which she covered herself as best she could.

The old priest watched that scene, inexplicable for him, with impatience. In fact, he had kept his promise, and he had come in his turn to ask the foreigners to accomplish theirs. He made them understand that the moment had come to play their role as a spirit outside, if they wanted to augment their ally's influence and acquire the means of finally getting off the island themselves.

But how were they to do that? It was necessary that Jeanne remain in the sacred grotto in order to escape the searches of the savages. On the other hand, it was necessary for the spirit to be able to manifest itself. They could not, however, abandon Jeanne on her own.

"One of us will stay here with you," said the two friends, in unison.

Which of them was to remain? Which of them was to go? Neither of the two had the courage to sacrifice himself voluntarily.

The old priest, who could have tipped the balance by choosing his acolyte of the first day, was very perplexed. He wondered whether it would be better to commence with the exhibition of the stronger or that of the cleverer.

"Jeanne," said Marius, courageously, "it's necessary for you to decide our fate. Whichever of us leaves might not come back. The one who remains, even if he dies in this grotto, will at least have the supreme joy of dying with you. Jeanne, you said one evening that you would choose between us yourself. I would never have dared remind you of that promise, but today, the circumstances require that you keep it. Jean and I both adore you, but we're ready for any sacrifice. You know what we have sworn; you can be sure that we will not fail. The one who will not have the joy of being preferred by you will have the consolation of devoting himself to the happiness of the other. Choose, Jeanne; it's necessary."

"Yes," added the Hercules. "It's necessary."

Jeanne was very embarrassed. She sensed simultaneously a kind of modesty in declaring her amour for one and a remorse for the pain she was about to cause the other, so she dared not affirm her choice overtly. For that choice was made, alas. And Marius perceived it clearly when he saw the young woman, almost ashamedly, without saying a word, go to take Jean Pioux by the hand.

Cruel anguish! Poor Marius! He is there, forehead inclined, arms dangling, body inert. He is thinking. He is thinking bitterly about everything for which he had hoped, everything that has flown away. He wants to pass through his mind repeatedly his sweet dreams of happiness, which are falling one by one, like dead flowers or shot birds.

He would have been so joyful, so happy, so good with Jeanne! He, the errant singer, the acrobat with neither hearth nor home, bronzed by all the suns of adventure, soaked by all the rains of Bohemia, tanned by all the winds of poverty, had arranged a charming life for himself in advance. In his imagination, he had placed the first stone of his hearth, collected the moss for his nest. He had seen himself calm, settled, devoted to his beloved wife, remembering his past acrobatics to amuse handsome little long-haired Mariuses. He had created an entire paradise for himself of autumnal amours, a sweet and melancholy garden with yellowed grass, great gilded trees and a luxuriously crimsoned sky.

And all that, all that joy, all that peace, in which to warm his weary body, that heart into which to pour out his own full heart, that adored wife, those cherished children, that glimpsed Eden, it was necessary to renounce. It was necessary to resign himself to resuming the solitary voyage, without a goal, without courage and without hope. From the happiness that he had encountered as a friend on the road, it was necessary to separate at the first turning.

Marius could not stand it. He burst into tears.

Oh, if Jeanne had said at that moment "I love you!" how he would have fallen into a sudden intoxication! How he would have replied to her:

"Come on, let's go! I'll find a means of enabling you to live, of defending you, of making you happy. I'm not afraid of anyone! I'll vanquish the whole world! I'll convince the whole world! I'll dance for the sun if necessary! I'll sing songs to the moon; I'll jump all the way to the clouds; I'll turn somersaults in the sky. Do you want me to filch two stars to make pendants for your ears, or the rings of Saturn to make you a ring? Say, order—I'm mad!"

And in passing from despair to that delirium, his heart would have burst like the heart of an oak swollen with sap.

But Jeanne did not say anything. She was still holding the hand of the Hercules, who lowered his eyes, almost ashamed of Marius' dolor.

He felt, in fact, that there was a sort of cowardice on his part in letting his friend suffer thus. He understood the grandeur of the sacrifice that was being demanded of Marius, and perhaps he would not have had the strength to accomplish it himself. On the other hand, however, seeing that Jeanne did not oppose it, he experienced in the depths of his soul a hidden joy that prevented him from doing anything.

Jeanne, for her part, found in that unsought circumstance the realization of her secret wishes. She loved Jean more than Marius. That was a fatality that she could not resist. Thinking about Marius' good humor, his devotion and the services he had rendered, she reproached herself for abandoning him. But what could she do? Had she not said that one day she would decide between them? Was not the one she would refuse prepared to receive the blow? Thus her mind reasoned, in order to appease the remorse of her heart.

Marius looked at them; he understood their attitude. He saw that he had nothing for which to hope. He sensed that Jeanne's silence for him was a declaration of love for

Jean. He told himself that in his friend's place, he would doubtless act as he was doing. He reminded himself of what they had promised the young woman. He repressed his tears, took hold of all his courage again, and advanced toward them.

"All right!" he said. "I can see that you love one another too much . . ."

Sobs broke his voice.

"Marius!" said Jeanne. "Don't weep, my good Marius!"

"Poor old fellow," said Jean, hugging him in his arms. "I'm very cowardly, aren't I?"

"No," replied the excellent man, "no. You're very fortunate, that's all."

And without pronouncing a bitter word, he followed the old sorcerer, who was getting increasingly impatient.

"No, no!" cried the old man, suddenly. "Spirit not dressed in *Oui oui*. Spirit all naked. Spirit tattooed."

Marius understood, and undressed behind the rock. He only kept a shred of a handkerchief in order not to be indecent in Jeanne's eyes.

"Adieu," he said to the couple who remained. "I'll console myself by working for you with all my strength."

"Marius," cried the young woman, "you're the best of men. You're good. Can you forgive us?"

"Forgive you for what? I don't hold anything against you, I swear. Here, the proof that I'm cheerful is that I've had an odd idea. Put my clothes on—that will be funny."

"And it will prevent me from getting cold, won't it?"

"And that will make me very glad," he added, going away with large tears in his eyes.

XV
Blood Wedding in a Tomb

JEAN and Jeanne were quite astonished to find themselves alone, together, free to talk to one another with an open heart. That liberty embarrassed them, and at first they could not pronounce a single word. Jean above all, more gauche in amour than in anything else, remained silent and almost cold, not knowing how to initiate the conversation, and yet wanting to tell Jeanne about all the joy he was experiencing. For her part, Jeanne thought, with reason, that she had already been only too clear in her demonstrations of amour; she judged that her choice was well worth thanks, and she expected those thanks. They were, therefore, two very embarrassed individuals.

With the marvelous art that women have for cutting through difficult situations, Jeanne found a means of starting the conversation.

"I'm scared!" she suddenly exclaimed.

"Scared of what?" asked the Hercules.

"Of everything that surrounds us. Look, up there, up there, see how it's shifting. It seems to me that there are beasts there. Don't you see it?"

And she pointed at the fissures in the coral, where the torchlight caused apparitions to dance and grimace.

But he did not look. He was not thinking about the grotto's phantasmagorias. In what Jeanne had said to him, he only saw one thing, which was that Jeanne had addressed him as *tu*. That new mark of amour caused blood to rise to his cheeks.

At the same time, he sensed Jeanne very close to him. Their hands were entwined; their breasts were touching. He counted all of his beloved's heartbeats; he was pressed by that charming, emotional cleavage that swelled and subsided alternately with delightful movements. He was burned by that contact; he plunged into the depths of her eyes; he drowned himself in amour in an ardent and mute ecstasy.

"Why aren't you replying to me?" Jeanne said

"But yes, I'm replying, I'm . . ." And he squeezed her in his arms in her turn.

That mute response was so energetic, so amorous, so full of desire, that Jeanne, familiar a moment ago, was almost afraid. She resisted his grip, and recoiled, saying; "Jean, what are you doing?"

"Oh," he cried, "for pity's sake, Mademoiselle Jeanne, don't be annoyed. Why aren't you saying *tu* any more? I was so happy! I was so proud! Think, then! From the moment when you declared, in sum, that you loved me, since that moment of intoxication, have I been able to tell you what I feel? Have I even been able to thank you? And now that we're alone, not that I can finally tell you everything, now that my over-full heart, heaped with all your bounty, is swollen with all my amour, dares to burst and open up to you, now . . ."

"Oh! Oh, my dear Jean," the young woman interrupted, "how loquacious you've become!"

"That's because I love you so much!"

"Well," she said, "and me, great child, don't I love you?"

And she tugged his beard, smiling.

"Oh, thank you, thank you, Mademoiselle . . ."

"What! Mademoiselle? I'm saying *tu* to you and you're saying *vous* to me!"

"Jeanne, my Jeanne, I love you!"

And their lips met in a kiss.

But once again, as if alarmed. Jeanne immediately recoiled. At the moment of yielding to all her womanly desires, she had been gripped again by all her maidenly modesty. And, sensing on her mouth the burning mouth of her lover, she had felt a frisson of fear at the same time as a frisson of amour. She feared that for which she hoped. It seemed to her that the wine of amour was rising too red and too intoxicating to the head of the Hercules.

"Let's be sage," she said.

They were, in fact, sage. A great silence fell. What could they talk about except their amour? But those silences only serve to blow on the fire that one wants to put out. For saying nothing, one does not think any less. On the contrary, one thinks more. Desires are excited in dreams.

After a few moments, in spite of their good resolution to be sage, they had drawn closer to one another again. Their hands interlaced without asking anyone's permission, and the young woman returned naturally to place her head in her beloved's breast.

During that period of silence, however, he had made a few sad reflections.

"My poor Jeanne," he said, hugging her in his arms, "what's going to become of us? Alas, I'm very much afraid . . ."

"Afraid! That's the first time, my dear Jean, that I've heard you pronounce that word!"

"And in fact, I've never been afraid, as long as it was a matter of me, and as long as I thought that I was big enough to stand up to all the dangers that might threaten you. But now, I don't know why, it seems to me that I can't defend you. If it's necessary for us to die of starvation in this grotto, what do you want me to do? I can't fight against that."

"That's not a reason to be afraid."

"Yes, I'm afraid for you, darling—for you, so young, so beautiful, exposed to such cruel adventures."

"Bah! We'll get out of it. You're a bird of ill omen. I, on the contrary, have happy presentiments. Marius will bring us provisions. We'll stay here for a week. Then, one fine night, we'll leave. And we'll find a means to leave the island. We'll go to Sydney, if you like."

"To Sydney? By what route, my love? On what ship, child?"

"We'll go, I tell you. I'm sure of it. The surrounding archipelagoes are full of coasters that trade with Australia. Someone will take us aboard. For one thing, you and Marius are excellent sailors, and I'll do the cooking for the crew, if necessary. But we'll leave, we'll go, we'll arrive. What joy! It seems to me that I'm already there."

"Oh, if that were true! Oh, yes, what joy! How happy we would be! How I would work, with all my strength, with all my heart! For I won't remain an acrobat, as you can imagine. I don't want you to be the wife of a performer. I'll take up a trade. I don't know any thoroughly, but I've begun to learn several. I could be a blacksmith, a wheelwright or a carpenter. I'm strong. I'll have courage.

Won't you be there to sustain me, to fortify me, to love me? What a good life we'll lead! When I come back from work in the evening, I'll find my Jeanne in the house, and my little Jeannettes and Jeannots, and in order to relax, I'll hug them all forcefully . . ."

"How your Jeanne will kiss you at that moment," the young woman replied, cutting off his speech with a kiss.

"Oh, Jeanne, oh, my adored, don't kiss me like that! It drives me mad. And then, you see, it reawakens my terrors. When I think of all the happiness that you're promising me, and of which I dream, it seems to me that it's too much, that it isn't possible, and that all that will vanish, and I see reality more frightful, and I'm afraid. Oh! To lose so many joys, is frightful! To have glimpsed the sky and to fall back into this darkness, to find oneself back in this tomb!"

"You're frightening me in your turn. What if it were you who's right! What if we're going to die here! Oh, I don't want you to die! I don't want to die! I want to live, with you! I love you! I love you!"

She pressed herself against him more recklessly. Their exhalations were confused, their limbs entwined; they were thirsty for one another.

"I'm afraid of dying," Jeanne repeated. And, leaning close to Jean's ear, she said to him quietly, very quietly, but in an ardent voice: "If we're going to die, before dying, I want to be yours!"

Jean replied with a mad embrace, with kisses punctuated by sobs, and among the sighs, the cries, the caresses, the tears and the bites, their two bodies fell, melted into one alone, on the red sand of the grotto.

That tomb was their nuptial chamber.

When they awoke from their stupor, the torch was almost extinct. From the ledge on which they had placed it, thick tears of resin were falling, drop by drop. The smoky light was vacillating, and caused palpitating shadows to dance on the ceiling. The entrance of the tunnel was shrouded in darkness.

"Oh," said Jeanne, "how dark it is! The light is dying! If Marius doesn't come back soon, we're going to be in darkness."

"I'll go to see whether there's another torch behind the rock," Jean replied.

"You're going to leave me here all alone?"

"Come with me, my dear—come on! In any case, it's there, only a few paces away."

"No, go! I'm not a coward. And then, I'm tired. I'd rather stay here, lying on the ground. I'll rest. I'll stay under the light. Just talk to me!"

She lay down nonchalantly, her back turned to the entrance of the grotto, watching her lover go back and forth, searching first under the anterior part of the rock.

"I can't see anything," said the Hercules, after a moment. "Perhaps it's on the other side. I'll look there. You're not afraid, my little Jeanne?"

As she did not reply he turned round, and saw that she was asleep. He blew her a kiss and went round to the other side of the rock, walking on tiptoe, avoiding stirring the pebbles in order not to wake her.

The silence of the grotto was only troubled by the distant murmur of the lake and the gentle and plaid respiration of the young woman. Once or twice it seemed to Jean that he heard a vague sound, but he paid no attention to it. It was doubtless a buzzing insect, a liana brushing the ceiling, or a ripple in the water splashing.

Jean was far from thinking of any danger. He was only thinking about pleasant things, the happiness that Jeanne had just given him, the future that present joy gilded with hope. The noise seemed to him like the breath of a kiss that had flown from Jeanne's lips to come and settle on his own.

Alas, it was Barbellez who had arrived.

He had departed with twenty-five of his men to search for his daughter and the escaped convicts at the same time. Thanks to the terror that his little troop inspired, and thanks also to the gifts that he made the savages, he had been informed first of Jeanne's abduction, and then her theft by the old priest. The old rogue himself, interrogated and threatened with death, had revealed the hiding place.

Fortunately for Marius, he had already quit the sorcerer's hut before the adjutant arrived. Curious by nature, and wanting to take advantage of his liberty to study the terrain, in order to see whether it might be possible to save themselves without the dangerous intervention of the old man, he had not returned directly to the grotto. In any case, he was weighed down by food supplies, torches, ropes and weapons, which slowed his progress.

Thus, Barbellez arrived before him. But the adjutant, in accordance with the words of the traitor who had sold the secret, was convinced that he was about to find the two escapees and his daughter in the trap.

He scarcely imagined that she was with them of her own free will. He thought, instead, in his brain of a prison guard habituated to see crime, that the two convicts had plotted to take possession of Jeanne in order to use her as a hostage in the case of misfortune.

Thus, he did not want to irrupt into the grotto with all his men.

Damn! he thought. *If my two fellows see that they're surrounded and certain to die, they might kill my daughter in order to avenge themselves. They're capable of it, the scum!*

He had, therefore, left his men at the entrance to the tunnel and had crawled all the way to the entrance of the grotto, only accompanied by the old priest. He was counting on his double-barreled rifle and his prodigious skill as a marksman to kill the two fugitives before they had time to suspect the danger.

"There's light in there, isn't there?" he asked his guide.

"Yes, yes; you'll see them, but they won't be able to see you."

"That's good. Softly, softly! Oh, the scoundrels! I'll catch them like rats in the bottom of a cooking-pot. I'll wager that I'll have them at the end of my rifle before they can say *oof*!"

He was not mistaken in his anticipations. As he arrived at the opening of the tunnel, hidden in the shadow, he saw by the trembling light of the torch that someone was lying close to the wall.

I recognize that costume, he thought. *That's evidently Marius. But where the devil is Jean? I'd like to see both of them, in order to fire my two shots reliably. That one's asleep. That's good. But where's the other?*

He made enough noise to attract the one who was hiding, but not enough to wake the sleeper.

This time, Jean heard perfectly, and even distinguished that the noise had come from the tunnel.

"Marius," he said, "is that you?"

And, emerging from behind the rock, he showed himself in the light in his turn.

Suddenly, a gunshot resounded. Jeanne stood up, uttering a heart-rending scream, and fell on her back. Jean, who had bounded toward her at her cry, received something like a blow of a fist in the chest and fell to his knees, also hit by a bullet.

At the same time, he heard someone leap into the grotto, crying: "Jeanne! Jeanne! My daughter! I've killed the wretches! Where are you?"

Jean got up, and found himself face to face with Barbellez.

"Your daughter!" he cried. "Look, murderer! She was wearing Marius' clothes. It's her that you've just killed . . ."

"Who? Where? My daughter!"

"There, there! On the ground. That's Jeanne."

As Barbellez leaned over her, Jean, mad with dolor, gathering his strength, swallowed the blood that was rising in his throat, took Barbellez by his two feet, and lifted him up in the air with a furious thrust.

Howling, Barbellez spun twice above the Hercules and went to flatten against the wall, where his crushed brain made a large white and red star.

Jean took a few more steps, tottering. Cold sweat soaked his temples. Bloody coughs shook his breast. Clouds passed before his eyes.

The torch went out.

"Jeanne, Jeanne," he stammered. "Where are you?"

And he searched in the dark with distraught gestures.

"Jean!" responded a faint voice. "Help! I'm going to die! Come!"

He ran in that direction, stumbling, his arms wide open, and fell beside Jeanne.

"Jean, my beloved," she whispered to him, in a dying voice. "Where are you? Kiss me! Kiss your little wife! My poor darling! I love you so much! Oh, I'm suffering! It seems to me that I'm going to choke! Kiss me, then!"

Jean hugged her weakly to his heart, whose beats were diminishing. He felt the life flowing out of him.

"Put your head on my breast," the young woman went on. "There! Rest! Are you suffering a great deal? You're not saying anything. Me, I need to talk, to talk more. I'd like to see you, to see your face, to see your eyes. I love you!"

Jean, already half torpid with death, woke up as he felt Jeanne's body stiffen convulsively. He no longer had the strength to speak, but he had enough to understand that it was the agony of death. He tried to raise his head, which was weighing on the young woman's breast. He wanted to utter a cry, to say a word, but the effort that he made finished him. A flood of blood filled his mouth and overflowed.

And Jean lay dead on Jeanne's cadaver.

XVI
The Death of Marius Mazuclard,
alias the Grasshopper

WHEN the old sorcerer had seen Barbellez killed he ran away precipitately

"Flee! Flee!" he had said to the soldiers. "The two convicts were shot by your chief, but he wanted to go into the grotto himself, and the bigger of the two men smashed his head against the wall. Now all three of them are dead."

"Barbellez is dead!" growled the sergeant. "Oh well, in truth, he hasn't stolen it. He was an old rogue."

"An old imbecile, too," added another. "He always wanted to know better than anyone else. He went in there on his own. It serves him right if he's copped it. Poor idiot! And when I think that he was strutting around yesterday in announcing his famous expedition to us!"

On that funeral oration, they left.

Half an hour later, when Marius arrived, there was no one at the tunnel entrance, and nothing revealed that anyone had been there, so he went into the subterranean passage.

He had salted fish, yams, taros and torches. There was enough to eat and to see clearly for a week. He also had two spears and three large cutlasses. That was for self-defense.

"They're going to be content!" he said.

Then, as he advanced, he added: "It's singular; there's no light visible at the end of the tunnel. A few rays ought to be arriving, though, since they have a lighted torch. Bah! Perhaps it's gone out. But I can't hear anything at all. Pooh! It's doubtless because they're talking in whispers."

Thus, Marius tried to explain all those worrying circumstances. In the depths of his heart, however, he was gradually invaded by a certain vague dread, and he increased his pace in the darkness.

He soon found himself at the interior mouth of the tunnel. There was indeed no light in the grotto.

A deathly silence floated there.

Are they asleep? he thought. *It isn't possible that any misfortune has overtaken them. What misfortune?*

And he shouted: "Hey, Jean! Jean Pioux! Mademoiselle Jeanne!"

The echoes replied to him, ironically.

"Have they gone? Oh, that isn't possible. Gone! Them, gone! Get away! They're not cowards. But then, in that case, they're dead! Oh, no! And them, dead without me! Oh, if they're dead, I'll kill myself too."

At that moment, he lit a torch, which illuminated the grotto. By its red and smoky light, Marius saw the three corpses lying close to the wall.

"Oh!" he cried, dully. "They're dead! But who's that dead with them? There's obviously been a battle, and I wasn't here! Wretch! Coward! It's necessary that I die! I want to be with them!"

The first cadaver that was in Marius' path caused him to recoil in horror. It was that of Barbellez, whose skull and face no longer formed anything but a mud of flesh, bone and blood. By the costume, Marius recognized the adjutant, and thus divined everything that had happened.

Further along were Jean and Jeanne, still in one another's arms, with Jean's head resting on Jeanne's breast.

Marius knelt down beside them slowly. The bodies were not yet cold, but they already had the inertia, both soft and rigid, that characterizes death. Marius understood that there was no more hope. He leaned over toward Jeanne and kissed her forehead. He took his friend's hand. Then, unable to contain his dolor, he burst into sobs, and remained thus, weeping, his head next to Jean's, on Jeanne's breast.

There, a thousand confused and incoherent reflections traversed his mind, a thousand memories and a thousand projects.

He tried to picture how they had died. He recalled various details of their speech or their habits, a word from Jean, a glance from Jeanne. He thought about what he was going to do.

What he was going to do? Alas, could he have the heart for anything, now? Would it even be possible for him to live? His disappointed amour had already depressed him greatly. But that lost amour would have been replaced by a long amity. What did it matter that Jeanne was Jean's? One could still sacrifice oneself for her, work for her happiness, have second place in her affections. Even if Jeanne had died alone, he would still have had Jean to love. But now, both of them being dead, nothing remained to poor Marius, nothing that could attach him to hope, render him courage, or tell him to live.

Then he told himself, again, that it was necessary to die.

An idea came to him, a crazy idea that he rejected at first, but which soon haunted him to the point of becoming an obsession. He dreamed of burying himself alive with the two beings that he had loved most in all the world.

But how to do it?

Marius had arrived at the degree of desperate grief that makes one lose one's reason and seek the most extraordinary, monstrous and sublime things coldly. He discussed with himself the various means of accomplishing his project.

An insensate inspiration suddenly illuminated his mind.

He picked up the torch, which he had thrown away and planted it on a spur of coral. Then he set to work. Having taken the bodies of Jean and Jeanne, he wrapped his ropes around them like bandages, in such a fashion that their arms could not be separated from one another. Then he put them on his back and, while he leaned them against a rock in order to maintain them in that position, he bound himself to them, at the shoulders and the neck. Thus, he was united with the two cadavers.

Then, buckling under the burden but nevertheless with a firm step, he advanced toward the lake, torch in hand.

Why the torch? He did not know. He marched like that, as if impelled by fatality. It was one of those moments when the crazed mind is no longer guiding the body, but allows itself to be dragged along by a breath of insanity.

He entered into the heavy black waves that glittered under the tawny light. He sank into them gradually, step by step.

When he had water up to his neck, he threw the torch away, which was extinguished with a hiss in the lake. Then he stopped for a moment, his eyes wide open in the darkness, his mouth smiling at the idea of death. A scrap of song passed through his mind, and as he let himself sink he sang, mechanically:

> *My sailor has fallen in the water!*
> *My sailor has fallen in the water!*
> *We only found his hat,*
> *And traderi tra la la la,*
> *We only found his hat,*
> *And traderi tra la la la,*
> *And traderi tra la la la.*
>
> *We only found his hat,*
> *We only found his hat,*
> *And his soul has gone over the water,*
> *And traderi tra la la la,*
> *And his soul has gone over the water,*
> *And traderi tra la la la,*
> *And traderi tra la lera.*

A PARTIAL LIST OF SNUGGLY BOOKS

LÉON BLOY *The Tarantulas' Parlor and Other Unkind Tales*

S. HENRY BERTHOUD *Misanthropic Tales*

FÉLICIEN CHAMPSAUR *The Latin Orgy*

FÉLICIEN CHAMPSAUR *The Emerald Princess and Other Decadent Fantasies*

BRENDAN CONNELL *Metrophilias*

QUENTIN S. CRISP *Blue on Blue*

LADY DILKE *The Outcast Spirit and Other Stories*

BERIT ELLINGSEN *Now We Can See the Moon*

BERIT ELLINGSEN *Vessel and Solsvart*

EDMOND AND JULES DE GONCOURT *Manette Salomon*

RHYS HUGHES *Cloud Farming in Wales*

JUSTIN ISIS *Divorce Procedures for the Hairdressers of a Metallic and Inconstant Goddess*

VICTOR JOLY *The Unknown Collaborator and Other Legendary Tales*

BERNARD LAZARE *The Mirror of Legends*

JEAN LORRAIN *Masks in the Tapestry*

JEAN LORRAIN *Nightmares of an Ether-Drinker*

JEAN LORRAIN *The Soul-Drinker and Other Decadent Fantasies*

CAMILLE MAUCLAIR *The Frail Soul and Other Stories*

CATULLE MENDÈS *Bluebirds*

LUIS DE MIRANDA *Who Killed the Poet?*

OCTAVE MIRBEAU *The Death of Balzac*

CHARLES MORICE *Babels, Balloons and Innocent Eyes*

DAMIAN MURPHY *Daughters of Apostasy*

KRISTINE ONG MUSLIM *Butterfly Dream*

YARROW PAISLEY *Mendicant City*

URSULA PFLUG *Down From*

DAVID RIX *A Suite in Four Windows*

FREDERICK ROLFE *An Ossuary of the North Lagoon and Other Stories*

JASON ROLFE *An Archive of Human Nonsense*

BRIAN STABLEFORD *Spirits of the Vasty Deep*

TOADHOUSE *Gone Fishing with Samy Rosenstock*

JANE DE LA VAUDÈRE *The Demi-Sexes and The Androgynes*

JANE DE LA VAUDÈRE *The Double Star and Other Occult Fantasies*

RENÉE VIVIEN *Lilith's Legacy*